Mrs. John Hodder Needell

Julian Karslake's Secret

Vol. 2

Mrs. John Hodder Needell

Julian Karslake's Secret
Vol. 2

ISBN/EAN: 9783337048464

Printed in Europe, USA, Canada, Australia, Japan

Cover: Foto ©Andreas Hilbeck / pixelio.de

More available books at **www.hansebooks.com**

JULIAN KARSLAKE'S SECRET

A NOVEL

BY

MRS. JOHN HODDER NEEDELL

'*It is open to us as a possibility, but closed against us as a right, to follow the lower when the higher calls*'

IN THREE VOLUMES

VOL. II.

LONDON

SMITH, ELDER, & CO., 15 WATERLOO PLACE

1881

CHAPTER XVI.

WHEN Sybil came down to breakfast the following morning Sara handed her a letter.

'Four days off duty have made me very un-
comfortable, my dear ; but now comes the explanation, and all will be right.'

Sybil took it with seeming composure, for
she knew Helstone's eyes were upon her, but
she felt the colour rise in her cheek and was
conscious of a quicker throbbing of her pulses.
She was full of extreme anxiety as to the pur-
port of that letter, an anxiety which a few

weeks ago she would have thought it impossible
any communication from Karslake could have
caused her.

Both host and hostess watched her while
she read it; the latter from the friendly desire
of discovering whether Sybil was pleased with
it, the former from the equally unmixed motive
of observing how she received what there might
be of dissatisfaction in it.   He saw that it was
very short and that she grew grave over the
perusal; also that she read it through a second
time before slipping it into the pocket of her
dress.   He waited for her to speak, but she
remained silent and preoccupied, without
glancing in his direction.   It was a relief when
his sister broke in impatiently.

'Well, Sybil, are we to hear nothing? are
not his excuses sufficient?'

'I believe he makes none, but he proposes
an excursion to Hampton Court, and asks if

you and I will meet him at the station at two
o'clock this morning. Will you be disposed ? '

Helstone interposed harshly. ' It is out of
the question ! you are under my protection,
Sybil, and I forbid it. I am prepared to give
you my reasons as soon as you please to listen,
but neither you nor Sara shall consort with this
man any more.'

Sara stared at him with blank amazement;
had it been night instead of morning she would
have thought him under the influence of wine;
as it was a vague doubt made her shiver—was
he losing his head?

Sybil seemed less surprised but very much
more displeased; there was a very calm but
resolute purpose in her tone as she replied, still
without looking at him :

' I am sure you will not lay any commands
upon me that I could not obey, or dissuade Miss
Helstone from giving us the pleasure of her

company. As soon as breakfast is over I shall
be glad to hear whatever you may have to say
to me.'

Helstone's swarthy cheek grew pale ; the
girl was already in opposition.

' Does this ——does this——' he hesitated ;
to forbear to pronounce Karslake's name without some opprobrious epithet required an effort
of self-command, one too which he perceived
from Sybil's now grave and steadfast look that
she fully perceived and understood.

' Does he write with the same assurance as
before, without any recognition of difference or
hindrance ? '

Sybil hesitated. ' Do you think it is quite
fair to either Mr. Karslake or myself to
ask these compromising questions, especially
before a third person and one who is his
friend ? Not,' she added quickly, turning
towards Sara with that sweet graciousness

which was so winning a charm, 'that there shall be any reserve between us, so soon as I know the meaning of all this. Just now a little misunderstanding has arisen, about which Mr. Helstone seems to know more than I; but I do not believe it to be serious.'

A look of almost superb scorn lighted up Helstone's face. Sybil encountered the expression and a burning colour dyed her face, the sensitive lips quivered a little. She turned to Sara.

'When Mr. Karslake parted from me at Burlington House last Friday, it was quite understood that a few days should elapse before we met again. In this note he tells me that Mr. Helstone has an important communication to make to me, but requests that, if possible, after having heard it we will meet him as I have told you.'

'If possible! Precisely so, the words are not ill-chosen, and I tell you it will not be possible.'

'On that point I reserve my right of private judgment. May I go into the drawing-room, Miss Helstone, and wait there till your brother is ready? I have not much zest for breakfast.'

She stood for a moment and drank the cup of coffee already poured out for her, and as she thus stood Helstone's eyes dwelt upon her with an admiration kindled and quickened by hope. The graceful poise of the tall slim figure, with its delicate and tender curves, the beauty of the face, full as it was of emotion and expression, touched every fibre of his being. Should this guileless and noble loveliness fall to the share of a traitor and a cheat? Never while the power of protest and exposure was his.

'I will follow you almost immediately,' he said, but before he could do so Sara called him back.

'Gilbert, I know your secret, and I want to

say just two words. You have heard some scandal about Mr. Karslake, and are going to take an advantage of it that in another man you would call infamous. Think twice before you meddle with what may turn out a more serious business than you expect. Mr. Karslake is not a man to be trifled with, nor, for that matter, is Sybil the girl.'

'I have heard no scandal,' he replied drily; 'what I am about to tell Sybil Dorrimore are matters of fact that have come under my own observation;' and he went out, leaving his sister staggered for a moment by so clinching a rejoinder.

He went straight to the window where Sybil stood awaiting him; there was something in the virginal calm and dignity of her aspect that checked for a moment the eagerness of his purpose.

'My child,' he said tenderly, 'you and I

have had many unconventional confidences before now : you will not hate me if what I am obliged to tell you hurts you very much ? '

' If you are obliged,' she said, ' there is no question before us, whether it hurts me or not.'

There was such a quiet air of unshaken confidence in her tone that it restored the former bitterness of his feelings. He turned from her and threw himself into a chair at a little distance.

' I did not tell you last Saturday that I struck work, feeling more unhinged by the events of the night than I ever remember to have done before, and that in order to kill the time I betook myself to the Crystal Palace. There, quite unexpectedly, I met your husband-elect. How long is it to the wedding-day, Sybil ? ' She turned and looked at him with a sort of pained surprise.

' I cannot bear to hear you speak of Julian

Karslake, not because you disparage him, but because you do such injury to your better self. As for our marriage, you know quite well the month of September is spoken of.'

' My God!' he exclaimed harshly, ' you try my temper more than I can bear.'

And then he told his story, deliberately, pitilessly; reproducing the scene as he thought with strict accuracy. But it was not so; he conveyed the idea of passionate response on Karslake's part towards the lovely woman weeping on his shoulder, whereas in point of fact his attitude had only been one of passive sufferance.

Sybil listened as a martyr may bear his torture; the blood rising and paling in her cheek, the eyes veiled and downcast, the interlaced fingers which had been hanging loosely before her, tightening gradually their repressive grasp; but offering no interruption

thought it was possible and have given him the opportunity—in vain!'

He went over rapidly his visit to the Rectory, detailing every damaging incident and presenting his own deductions from them as if they had been facts rather than impressions. Once or twice Sybil made a movement of interruption or inquiry, but checked it; she was very pale but he saw from expression and attitude she had taken her resolution.

'Is that all—at last?' she demanded. 'You have closed your case? You can at least have seen or heard nothing since last night?'

'I have nothing more to add,' he replied sternly, 'except to renew my protest against your meeting Karslake to-day. It would not be seemly, it would scarcely be womanly, but you do not think of it?'

Sybil smiled bitterly. 'You forget I have had to take care of my own honour and welfare

since I was a child, and am scarcely likely to
accept dictation in a matter like this. I shall
meet him to-day according to his arrangement,
and I hope for my sake you will allow Sara to
go with me. It is hardly likely Mr. Karslake
and myself will return together.'

A spasm of anguish constricted her heart as
she spoke, induced, she thought, by the keenness
of the sense of her outraged dignity and faith;
for if love betrayed had caused the pang, she
would have refused to acknowledge it even to
her most secret consciousness.

'He does not expect it,' urged Helstone,
'even he puts it as a contingency more than
doubtful. "If possible:" that is, if you can
stoop so low as to hear and see him again.'

'I would not condemn my worst enemy un-
heard, still less one who stood in so close a relation to all of us as Mr. Karslake does. Would
it be reasonable to refuse him the opportunity

of speech in a matter that is almost more than life or death to each of us?'

'To each?'

'Yes; you must think me strangely insensible if such a blow as this is to be struck upon my faith in human nature and leave no trace. You will let me go now, please; I must have a little time to collect my thoughts.'

He got up and opened the door for her his eyes following her with a passionate yearning pain. If he had not been checked by the certainty of her indignant contempt at such a crisis, he could have fallen on his knees before her and begged her to take pity on his love.

CHAPTER XVII.

IT was a sultry morning, the first day of August; the heat was oppressive to exhaustion in town, but would only enhance the enjoyment of the green swards and sylvan alleys of Hampton Court Gardens. What outlet could be more delightful for lovers in their heyday of passionate altruism, and so richly endowed with all that could give additional charm and zest to life?

Something like this were the questions Sara Helstone was asking Sybil a few hours later, kindly bent on bringing back a smile to her lip and a little colour to her pale cheek, also on superintending her toilette and preventing her from making a guy of herself because she was in trouble.

Her own faith in Karslake was unshaken. Helstone had departed for town without vouchsafing her any explanation, and her own good feeling withheld her from questioning Sybil, either directly or indirectly. To render such forbearance easy she was to be her companion, and would be able to make her own observations and draw her own conclusions.

'Do not consider me in the least, my dear,' she said to her as they walked slowly towards the station. 'I have a novel in my pocket and so soon as we get to a shady seat all I shall ask is to be left alone with it. But do you think it wise to look so pale?' she added, tapping her hand affectionately.

'I look as I feel,' said Sybil, smiling down gratefully upon her friend.

'And you are pretty enough to dispense

with colour.   I never flatter, but you look as if
you had stepped out of some old canvass—say
of Titian or Vandyck—with all the warm tints
mellowed and harmonised by age.'

The praise was not exaggerated; the girl
wore a black dress of some thin texture over
silk of the same colour, draped with almost
Grecian severity; some adjustment of muslin
and lace about her shoulders, which had the
tint of old ivory, and a broad brimmed Leghorn
hat with white feathers and black velvet.

'You have spoiled your pretty costume with
that ugly sunshade,' remarked Miss Helstone
again, seeming to think conversation necessary
to keep up her companion's spirits. 'Where is
the dainty toy Julian Karslake brought you the
other day? Has it gone so far that his gifts are
tabooed?   Well, this is our platform, and there
he is now to speak for himself.   I never saw
him in a grey morning suit before; how well

he looks in it! but then nature has ordained he must look well in anything.'

Until that moment when her eyes fell upon him, Sybil had under-estimated the anguish of the situation. Her colour changed rapidly, her pulses beat with excitement. Would he venture to approach her with that sweet dignity of mien to the charm of which she had never been insensible, and hold out his dishonoured hand? What was implied—woman-like she asked herself—in the unusual style of his dress? did it mean a tacit abrogation of functions of which he had been proved unworthy?

He was at the farther end of the platform as they stepped upon it, and had all the distance to measure beneath the easy scrutiny of the one woman, and the veiled observation of the other; undoubtedly there was a measure of constraint in his manner, and as he came nearer Sybil saw the large-lidded blue eyes looked

14

darker and heavier, and the slight habitual
tension of the level brows was deepened into a
fixed contraction.   No one looking into his face
could fail to see there was the repression of
pain in it, but the shamed humility of the
criminal was wanting.

He shook hands with Miss Helstone first,
who advanced effusively to meet him,
anxious to show there was no change in her
feelings towards him.   Then he turned to Sybil
with a luminous smile that banished all the
shadows from his face, and was as far removed
from deprecation as possible.

'I knew you would come,' he said, 'but
none the less am I grateful for your coming.   I
ask nothing more at present.'

He did not touch her hand, but his glance
conveyed such tender admiration as must be
hard, thought Sara, for any girl's heart to resist.

'I will take our tickets for East Molesey,'

he said, ' for the heat in the train will be suffocating, and then we will take the water and row
up the river as far as you please.'

Sybil so far forgot the situation as to allow
her face to brighten at this announcement, but
it fell again immediately. She ensconced herself
in the remotest corner of the railway-carriage,
and looked steadily, with averted head, out of
the window. It was a relief to her that
Karslake considerately placed himself on the
same side, so as to spare her the embarrassment
of his regard, and made no attempt to draw her
into conversation. But the brief journey soon
came to an end, and then as the three were
bound to walk together for a time through the
leafy lanes and fields of East Molesey, the
restraint that weighed upon them all became
more irksome.

' Look here ! ' said Miss Helstone, suddenly
stopping short and facing round on Karslake in

her abrupt but friendly fashion, 'I know it
must be hard work to be talking civil platitudes
to me when your mind is full of other things.
Put me out of consideration entirely, and fall
back with Sybil and have it all out at once.
My theory in life is never to carry a burden a
step further than necessary.'

'You are very good : I did not quite know
that you understood so perfectly the position of
affairs,' replied he, with a slight inflection of
annoyance in his voice, 'but what I have to say
could scarcely get said between this and the
river ; it is only a few steps now to the place
where we shall find the boat.'

He led the way till a turn in the path they
were following disclosed the river, winding
between its lovely wooded banks. A charming
little Thames pleasure-craft, with luxurious
cushions and awning, was moored to the willow
boughs that drooped over the steps of one of

the many little landing stages of the neighbourhood. The man in charge, half asleep in the
drowsy sunshine, roused and sprung out as they
approached.

'You are not afraid to trust yourself to me,
I hope?' said Karslake, smiling as he saw some
hesitation on Sara's part. 'The river is smooth
as glass, we are beyond the swirl of the
steamers, and, to add to your confidence,
I must tell you that I have pulled an oar
on two occasions as one of the 'Varsity eight!'

Sybil, who had already sprung into the boat
and taken her place with a feeling of perfect
security, looked up. He had thrown off his coat
and settled to his work, with one easy sweep of
the oars propelling the light craft far out into
the smooth current. He looked the very pro-
totype of youthful vigour and comeliness, but
some subtle and indefinable feeling rendered
the very charm of his aspect and his easy con-

ventional manner an offence to her perceptions. He seemed at once to baffle and displease her.

'Spare us,' she said in a low tone, 'any further disclosure of your merits; what we know already is as much as we can bear.'

She would fain have recalled the words the moment they had passed her lips—she hated herself for having thus spoken—but it was too late. Karslake crimsoned all over face and throat; the very hands that grasped the oars—and she could see how he tightened his hold of them—grew red, but he held his peace. It would have been a relief to her sense of keen compunction had he thrown her an indignant or reproachful glance. But if his face expressed anything, when he was resolutely bent on controlling expression, it was grieved surprise.

'What we know already!' repeated Sara, with rather too obvious an effort to cover the mutual embarrassment; 'Sybil's saucy words might stand as the text of our modern speculations ; they are the moot question of the day. I have often wished to ask you, Mr. Karslake, what you thought of all this agnostic controversy. I lead a dull life, and read a great deal.'

He looked up after a moment, and smiled at the kindly speaker.

'I fear I am not an expert in the tenets of the school, but I suppose it is the inevitable outcome of dogma without faith, and of the fatal tendency to divorce reason from religion. An inflexible belief is perhaps a lost possibility to our age.'

'But does not your esteemed Dr. Newman hold an inflexible belief?'

'Who knows? at least he has secured it under the padlock of infallibility.'

Sybil scarcely followed what they said ; her whole mind was bent upon drawing conclusions from every look, or word, or gesture that escaped him. Was it possible that treachery and imposture could take so consummate and gracious a form? but then again the essence of the charge against him was that his duplicity had been so complete and unsuspected.

' Shall we keep to our original intention and get out here ?' he asked presently ; ' this is the nearest point to the gardens.'

Sara assented, and as no direct appeal had been made to her opinion Sybil remained silent.

She would willingly have protracted the water-course indefinitely, dreading the. ordeal before her with an intensity of pain and distress that increased as the inevitable moment drew nearer.

However, there was no alternative. Karslake pulled the boat close to the bank and held it firm while she first sprung on shore, and then turned to assist Miss Helstone, who performed

the feat as ungracefully as do nine women out
of ten under the same circumstances. But this
arrangement precluded the necessity of Karslake
offering her his hand. He moored the boat
firm to a post sunk in the bank, and a few
minutes more brought them within the royal
enclosure.

'It is not a free day for the palace,' he said,
now directly addressing Sybil, 'even if you
cared to explore it. There is very little interest inside of it, barring a few insipid portraits,
and our object to-day is not to look at pic-
tures. I have a pass for the private gardens
if Miss Helstone would prefer them, and for
the rest, will you walk with me in another
direction? I know the grounds thoroughly,
and can find a place where we can talk undis-
turbed.'

Sybil looked at the chestnut shaded bench
on which her friend had taken her seat, having

declined the offer of the seclusion of the private
gardens and already drawn forth her volume
from her pocket, with a strong desire to place
herself beside her and postpone the painful
interview that impended; but Karslake stood
awaiting her instant obedience as it seemed,
without the possibility of objection or refusal
on her part having occurred to him.

'And how should it occur to him?' she
asked herself, 'when the one object that has
brought us together is that I may hear what he
has to say to me?'

For all that she rose slowly and with evident reluctance; so obvious was it that, when
they had moved a few paces out of ear-shot,
Karslake stopped and said:

'Are you repenting already that you have
consented to meet me to-day? I was more
grateful for your goodness than words can express, but some change of feeling on your part

seems to have taken place. I do not blame you. Shall I take you back at once to Miss Helstone and say what is necessary by letter? I would rather have spoken, but if it is disagreeable to you—as who can wonder?—my personal wish counts for nothing.'

He spoke not only with that silvery clearness of utterance and absolute composure of manner, which had often jarred before upon the girl's eager and sensitive nature, but there was an unquestionable restraint and disappointment of tone that seemed to her out of place in their mutual relations.

She lifted up her eyes, alight with indignation and pain.

'Is the matter before us one of choice or inclination?' she asked, 'or can you fail to understand how much of personal feeling I must have sacrificed to my sense of what justice to you demanded? It is as much as I can bear to hear you coolly propose delay, as if such a thing were possible in a case like this.'

He looked at her earnestly; not so much with tenderness or sympathy as with the long, sustained gaze of one bent on solving a doubtful problem, and who accepts the solution at all costs.

'Pardon me,' he said gently, 'there shall be no delay; but I find we cannot talk here, every passer-by turns and looks at us. We will go to the private gardens ourselves, where we shall escape the glare of the sunshine.'

He turned, and she walked by his side in silence; walked with a haughty erectness of gait and a hard set expression on her face, of which she was scarcely conscious, but after the long look of searching inquiry he had not glanced at her again.

They passed before the long façade of the

quaint old structure, standing out in sharp relief
against the radiant azure of the sky, every brick
of which seemed to glow and radiate heat in
the sultry, oppressive atmosphere. Karslake
showed his pass to the lazy official half asleep
on his bench beside the entrance-gates, and
then they were free of the delicious greenery of
those gardens which are perhaps the most
charming and complete specimen of the Dutch
taste in Europe. He led the way to a certain
thick-pleached alley with which he was acquainted, where the light came cooled and softened through branches trained and interlaced
for centuries, and the turf beneath their feet
was a vivid and elastic carpet, velvet piled.
There, too, was a comfortably cushioned bench,
on which he placed Sybil with that sweet and
courteous solicitude for her comfort which,
though habitual to him, seemed to her now an
ironical mockery of the momentous issues

between them.   He himself declined to sit
down.

'The criminal stands before the judge,' he
said with a slight smile, 'and such it seems are
our relations to each other.   I own, Sybil, I
had no sense of them when I came to meet
you to-day, and I see you have missed in my
manner the humility and anxiety you expected.
Shall I tell you what I expected?'

He took off the soft felt hat he wore and
threw it on the ground at his feet, and for a
moment passed his hand over his forehead with
a gesture difficult to define, but which seemed
to indicate a sense of weariness, not so much
the outcome of the present moment as of the
long experiences of the past.

'I asked you in my note of this morning to
come if it were possible; did you think the
words meant that, after having heard Mr.
Helstone's story, your reception of it would

create the difficulty? Ten thousand times no! I expected nothing from you but the more or less indignant repudiation of his slander, and the prompt action of a generous nature to assure me of your unshaken belief in my honour. The only fear in my mind was that he might succeed in coercing your inclination. Now I perceive that I was all wrong—utterly and miserably wrong—in those expectations, so much so that nothing occurs to me to say but to ask you what motive induced you to come at all?'

'Surely,' replied she in a low agitated tone, for every word that he spoke was an appeal to the chivalry of her nature, 'surely you were unreasonable in your expectations? It is not some idle gossip of society which has reached my ears, but the statement of a fact attested by one in whose integrity I have perfect confidence. I am come here, in defiance of his protest, to

give you what I think is the right of every man
—the opportunity of clearing your character
from injurious charges. I own,' she added,
with a burning blush, 'that my confidence in
your being able to do so, fell far below your
own estimate of what ought to have been my
feeling in the matter.'

' And suppose,' he answered, ' I tell you that
I deliberately refuse to clear my character from
these accusations—or rather, for I wish to hide
nothing, that I am absolutely unable to do so—
what then? Now, as before, when my loyalty
and good faith have been under discussion, I
have nothing but my bare word to produce for
the satisfaction of your doubts. I am constrained to confess that I have no explanation
to give of the incident of Saturday: if my
silence on the subject is accepted by you as
proof of my guilt——'

He stopped abruptly, his eyes dwelling
on the fair bowed face, and the quivering

and contraction of the lines round the lovely, sensitive mouth. An expression of passionate, but
hopeless yearning gathered slowly into his gaze.

'Perhaps you are right,' he said sadly, 'and
I am mad to expect that your belief in my
rectitude should withstand the weight of Mr.
Helstone's evidence. I own I had credited you
with a finer gallantry of temper than most women
possess: I thought, too, my life would have
spoken for me, and you would have recoiled
from the suggestion of such absolute baseness,
as I should have done had a slur rested on your
fair fame.'

'The cases are not parallel,' was her reply.
'I do not know enough of your real life to
depend upon its outward testimony, and as I
have said before, this is not a slur—a breath of
opinion. Why do you refuse to take into consideration that this is not an accusation based
upon suspicion but upon facts?'

He smiled bitterly. 'And I will ask you to take into consideration the medium of prejudice and personal enmity through which your eye-witness gazed and beheld these facts. Bear with me a moment if I recall the situation in its simple reality; a woman in sore distress leaning against me for support, and a little child standing by my side and demanding the meaning of his mother's grief. Simply the deductions he drew were false. I find it hard to say even so much as this, but I have nothing further to add to my absolute denial.'

Then there was a pause between them. Sybil sat with her arm on the padded elbow of her seat and her averted head bent upon her hand. The situation was exquisitely painful both to her tender maidenly reserve and to her womanly pride; a conflict of feeling stirred within her. While the attraction which Karslake exercised had never been so potent, her spirit of reason and independence rebelled against what seemed to her the almost tyranny of his requirements. Perhaps some subtle magnetism conveyed this impression to his mind, for he broke the silence by saying :

'You think I ask too much? I ask you, standing to me in the relation of promised wife, to accept implicitly my solemn assurance of unsmirched honour, and if this is more than you can do—and I know you will speak all the truth about it—then nothing remains but the rupture of our engagement. Do you remember my once telling you that without you life would not be worth living, and I should have no more zest for duty? Well, I do not say that now, although my love for you has strengthened since then ; but the worth of a life after all is not to be measured by the happiness enjoyed, and may very well be lived with all the high lights and warm colours washed out of it. I have never felt quite sure of getting you, Sybil, as a man is apt to fear to miss the prize on which he has staked his best. I have loved you, too, in that sort of fashion which does not often meet with adequate response or fulfilment.'

'Also in that fashion,' she answered, raising a proud, reproachful glance, 'which withholds confidence while demanding implicit belief. What proof have I of the strength of a love which is too feeble to break through all this painful mystery and reserve? I must, indeed, be dear to you when you will not forego your pride for my sake, and choose to cast me off rather than satisfy my most reasonable requirements!'

'Sybil, my love, my darling!' he said, with an impulsive movement towards her, which he checked however almost immediately, 'how am I to answer you? My love for you is the one love of my life—you are now, at this moment, as you have been the last three years, the wife of my desire. I have kissed no woman's lips, nay, no woman's hands but yours: try and believe this, and then ask yourself if it is possible that I could let any mere question of pride or personal injury stand between us? Instead of doubting the reality of my love, consider what must be the stress of circumstance to which I am bound to sacrifice it.'

'If it is something so grave and solemn as you imply,' she answered passionately, 'it only adds force to my plea that you should trust me with the truth. Do you fear that I am too weak to keep an honourable secret, or to share a burden that you must carry?'

Karslake's resolution must have been superhuman had it not for a moment faltered under the tender pathos of her appeal.

'Is she not right? should I not do well to trust

her?' was the prompt temptation that assailed
him. There was a brief breathless pause,
during which he revolved the question in his
mind with a desperate hope that reason or conscience would return a different verdict from
before, and Sybil watched the conflict of his
mind with an eagerness that checked the beat-
ing of her pulses. Then he turned and came
close to her, the beauty of his face exalted to a
sensible influence by the power of its expression.

'One of us must yield,' he said in a low
passionate tone, 'and it must be you, Sybil, for
I dare; not nor, on the other hand, will I
give you up without a struggle. If I had
not fought this battle in advance you would
have conquered me. Understand, my choice
lies between honour and dishonour, between
love and shame: yours is simply a question of
faith, more or less. If you will not deal out the
larger measure I must of necessity let you go—

that surrender is just possible to me—but it would be impossible to live under my own contempt or the shadow of your suspicion. Be generous, then—you to whom generosity has been so easy, and trust me utterly, now and for ever!'

He bent towards her suddenly, snatching both her hands in his, and straining his lips upon them.

'God knows,' he murmured, 'it would be easier to give up life than you? Will you go? surely, surely you must love me a little?'

Sybil looked up, stirred and thrilled with a passionate sympathy unknown to her before. Her eyes swimming with responsive tenderness met his, her light flexible fingers returned the strong pressure of his own.

'Not a little,' she answered, 'more I fear than is either wise or well.'

'My darling, my darling,' he whispered; and

then he sat down beside her, and for a few moments time ran unmeasured, and care had no existence.

He was the first to arouse himself with a painful sense of a duty half done.

'And when you go back to Burnham Square, how will you satisfy Mr. Helstone's inquiries? Do you quite realise that even to you, my love, my wife, I have no explanation to give—not a syllable to add to my naked disclaimer? that you yield yourself to me under these hard conditions?'

She looked at him steadily, with a gaze that seemed to reach his soul, but he endured the solemn scrutiny unflinchingly.

'I do,' she said. 'I believe in you with an inflexible belief, though surely never was a woman's faith so strained before!'

CHAPTER XVIII.

A MONTH later Julian Karslake was married to Sybil Dorrimore in the old parish church at Roosden Magna. It was a very quiet wedding; the bride had no crowd of attendant maidens about her, or interested friends watching every manifestation, and criticising every arrangement. One carriage took her and her father and the three younger children from Ashlands to the church, which was filled with as many of the rural population of the village as could manage to spare the time, and a few select stragglers whom curiosity had attracted.

She walked very slowly up the aisle leaning on her father's arm, who was conscious of an unusual sensation of complacency as he looked at the tall slight figure at his side, clothed in grey from hat to heel, and looking lovelier in her quiet pale emotion than he had ever thought her before. But then the aureole of her married dignity was round her head.

The three little children clustered about her, in their simple but pretty attire, as a body-guard, Lucy pressing close against her sister in defiance of all formality, in order not only to fulfil her delicate function of bridesmaid, but to make quite sure that Sybil was not crying; Bertie, who also had his misgivings, fixing Karslake with a round-eyed gaze of half shy, half defiant curiosity.

The bridegroom with his imperative friend— a well-bred stranger whom no one knew and everyone seemed to ignore—had been waiting at the altar fully twenty minutes before the arrival of the bride, and it was noticed by many with what an expression of intense anxiety he watched her slow progress to his side. But it was also observed that when this position was reached and the eyes of each encountered the other in involuntary greeting, the expression in his face was that of passionate inquiry, and in hers of grave and tender response. She even covertly stretched out her hand towards him, which he clasped and retained unbidden while the old vicar slowly droned through the time-honoured service, which surely challenges the revision of this age of reason and culture.

The ceremony over and all formalities duly observed, Sybil had to make her loving adieux to the dear little household band who, in spite of Mr. Dorrimore's impatient reprimands, clung sobbing round her skirts. She herself was not much given to bootless tears, but none the less her pale eloquent face showed how much she suffered, and her last words to her

father, before re-entering the carriage which
was to take her and her husband at once to the
station, were—

'For my sake be good to them—don't let
them be afraid of you!'

The marriage had been accomplished in
spite of the active and persistent opposition of
Gilbert Helstone.

Sybil had returned home to Ashlands, with
the full permission of her sympathetic hostess,
the day following the incidents at Hampton
Court. On that occasion she had simply an-
nounced to Gilbert her renewed and unshaken
belief in her lover, and had refused to listen to
protest or expostulation on his part.

He had felt driven to despair by her infatuation; it seemed to him incomprehensible—a
judicial blindness, nay, an almost diabolic prepossession. His first idea had been to go down
with her into the country and tell his story to

her father, and rouse up what there might be of manhood left in his nature ; but he decided it would be in vain.

Mr. Dorrimore believed in his future son-in-law to an extent that would make him impervious to suspicion, much more conviction, and he had a supercilious contempt for Helstone's opinions. To this would be added the potent influences of self-interest, and the force of his daughter's deluded purpose. He would do no good in this direction. But there were other ways ; he might investigate the scandal and bring such proofs of Karslake's double-dealing as should convince doubt and credulity, and to this end he must endeavour to trace the woman whom he had seen with him.

During the three weeks that elapsed before the wedding he inserted obscure but catching advertisements, daily, in three of the leading newspapers, varying their character and phraseology with an ingenuity that seemed exhaustless, and spending upon the experiment a great deal more than he was able to afford.

He had observed the details of both appearance and dress in mother and child with instinctive professional acuteness, and indicated his clue in a manner that could not have been missed had the appeals ever come under the eye for which they were intended; but there was no response. The only satisfaction he was able to extract from the proceeding was the idea of the annoyance and anxiety they must excite in Karslake's mind, for there was no doubt of his both seeing and comprehending them.

Indeed, on this point his certainty was confirmed in an unexpected manner: he met Karslake at King's Cross station about a week before his wedding day, and was surprised to see him approach with the evident intention of speaking. He himself was on the point of turning his back upon him contemptuously, but the thought that he might gather something to help his purpose induced him to alter his mind.

'You have something to say to me?' he asked with look and accent of studied insult.

Karslake returned the gaze with his usual quiet but complete self-command, which could not, however, conceal the fact that he was looking pale and harassed.

'Yes,' he said. 'I have a request to make. If you should have any reply to your advertisements, will you inform me of the fact? Not, I need scarcely say, with any view of influencing your action in the matter, but simply that I may know the ground I stand on.'

Helstone surveyed him with an expression of contemptuous surprise.

'Do you think me fool enough to stultify

the object I have in view? forewarned is fore-
armed.   Come ! you have succeeded in doing
what I should have said was impossible,—
increased my bad opinion of you.   Have you
turned coward as well as traitor ? '

'What I ask,' returned Karslake without
the slightest change of manner, ' is a bare point
of justice or at least of honour.   You are bent
on my ruin—of course with the inflexibility of
righteous condemnation.   I demand that you
do not strike in the dark; that you give me
warning of the steps you may be led to take
towards this end.'

Helstone's dark face paled with excess of
passionate feeling.

'Take the warning on the spot,' he
answered harshly ; 'I shall never give you any
other !   You have got what you wanted—the
noblest, sweetest creature on God's earth, and
all that now remains for me to do is to try that

her eyes may be opened, and to take her from you in the end, though I have failed in the beginning. Am I likely to help you to baffle me?'

He did not consider that he was betraying his own secret, or perhaps he disdained to do so, until he saw that Karslake's face expressed a sort of surprised pity which, in his present mood, irritated him almost to madness.

'For God's sake spare me your damnable sympathy and go, having your answer! At all costs, I count my honest loss better than your shameful gain, and no weakness of compassion towards the woman I love will prevent me from carrying out my purpose. When the time comes, as come it will, I shall choose for her misery rather than disgrace.'

He stopped, glanced at his companion keenly, and added with a sneer:

'You don't look a very jocund bridegroom,

your courage fails; else, why this change of face?
Your perjuries of a week or two back could
not have lacked unction; why do you come to
me now with a tacit admission of your guilt
and a squeak for mercy on your lips? It is
not quite too late—I will offer you another
chance. Give up your claim even now at the
eleventh hour to Sybil Dorrimore, and I will
drop my persecution. Leave her alone, and
you may pose to the end of the chapter as saint
and angel for what I care. You hesitate? Is it
possible?'

'I hesitate as to whether it is worth while
to try and disarm your enmity, and set your
judgment right in this matter, and that not
from any personal apprehension but in consideration of your kindness to the Ashlands family.
When I saw you last I could not bring myself
to deny your infamous conclusions. You know
I have done this since, and I will do the same

again. Is it quite hopeless that you should be induced to believe I speak the truth?'

He spoke with a natural reluctance but still without hesitation or slur of word or phrase, and Helstone felt himself baffled by an equanimity that it was out of the power of his outrages to shake. Perhaps it was the sense of this that added a sharper venom to his reply.

'After all,' he said, 'you lack the spirit of the full villain and have not the courage of your infamy. But reserve your pathos for the pulpit, and your protestations for the women you have deceived. To cheat me out of the conclusions of my eyesight is hopeless. Good morning.'

He turned on his heel and was going when a thought struck him.

'I guess there is not much love lost between us, though I give you credit for an amount of self-control no honest man would

care to display.   Console your hatred with the
idea that, in marrying Sybil Dorrimore, you will
put an end to a friendship that has been the
solace of a hard life before it became a passion
and a regret.   Don't wonder if I curse the day
on which your eyes first fell on her sweet face.'

' Will you be leaving the neighbourhood ? '
asked Karslake.

Helstone's eyes sparkled with anger.

' Were you going to suggest a more con-
venient locality—a safer distance from yourself
and her ?   Too many ties bind me to my present home to make it easy to leave it, and the
last will not be the weakest—the need of
keeping up a surveillance over your movements.'

Karslake smiled a little contemptuously ; an
angry rejoinder had risen to his lips but he
checked it, as it almost seemed in compassion
to his companion.   Instead he answered :

'I shall never try to put any pressure upon Sybil's inclinations; if she should still wish to keep up her friendship with you and Miss Helstone she will be free to do so.'

'Free to visit at our house without penalty or protest from you?'

'Free absolutely from any restriction on my part.'

Helstone looked at him curiously. 'In what light am I to view the concession? as a covert bribe to condonation?'

'You are at liberty to view it in whatever light you find most satisfactory; only in giving this permission to my wife, it is in the belief that all your instincts of honour and manhood are not buried under your hatred to me.' He made a slight gesture of leave-taking, and turned away too quickly to give his companion the chance of reply.

A few days later Gilbert Helstone sat in his

chambers with the announcement of the marriage in the 'Times' open on the table before
his eyes, and though he uttered no sound nor
showed any sign of feeling, the iron of irre-
vocable disappointment was entering his soul.
Had he ever loved her as he loved her at that
moment, when nothing was left him but absolute
loss and futility? Did the past ever rise before
him in reminiscence more cruelly distinct and
tender?

He thought of her as the lovely child who
had sat on his knee in the old Queen Street
nursery; as the growing girl seen, watched,
admired from year to year, as the fine possibilities of her nature ripened and developed.
Her gallant endurance of the manifold hardships
of life, her high-minded indifference to common
pleasures and loving devotion to the interests of
her family; the brightness of her spirit, the
sweet womanliness of her nature—he dwelt

upon it all as plea and justification of his own
idolatry. But a lover, however mature or
reasonable, does not dwell alone upon the moral
and mental endowments of his queen. To
Helstone's inward gaze Sybil stood before him
in all the sweet perfection of her physical beauty.
He knew every line of her tall, lithe figure,
every feature and turn of her face; the sweep
of the heavy braids of hair from the delicate
straight brows, the habitual look of radiant
softness in the large tender eyes, the pale bloom
of the clear skin, the warm crimson of
the perfect mouth, were as present realities to
the keenness of his introspective vision. He
recalled the latest expressions he had seen in
that vivid countenance; the indignant protest with which she had encountered his
accusations, the passionate zeal with which
she had afterwards defended her own faith
in her lover; the eyes suffused with ten-

der friendship as she had bidden him and
Sara farewell at the railway station ; the lingering touch of the small, brown, ungloved fingers.

As he sat with folded arms and lowering
brows thinking about it all, he knew that every
grace and charm, each endowment and capacity
was henceforth invested with a new potency of
allurement—the mad craving for the unattain-
able. His love for Sybil Dorrimore had been a
holy affection ; his passion for Sybil Karslake
was an inordinate hunger of the soul. And
then his mind slowly and reluctantly took up
the idea of the man who was the present and
inalienable possessor of all these adorable per-
fections. There had always been an instinctive
antagonism between them, but circumstances
had intensified the feeling into a reasoned and
deliberate principle. Helstone religiously believed in his own suspicions, and in so doing
was justified in the strength of his reprobation

and disgust. The known respect, not to say admiration, in which the other was regarded by the world, the charm of his person and manner, the characteristics of his individuality—in which there was so subtle an attraction that he was not wholly insensible to it himself—only served to exasperate the sense of his real worthlessness.

He had failed miserably to open Sybil's eyes to the truth ; on the contrary, the attempt had stimulated her languid regard by appealing to the chivalry of her nature.

'Poor girl,' he thought with tenderest pity, ' not all her gifts of mind and intellect availed to save her from the extremity of feminine infatuation. But when the illumination comes, when it is in my power to put the proofs of her husband's guilt before her, how will her boundless indignation and scorn, and the completeness of her repudiation, avenge that period of delusion ! '

Well, he would work for this end ; to the outside world he was nothing beyond the plodding professional man, making fair headway at the bar by dint of a certain reliable astuteness, but with no aptitude for brilliant successes, no characteristics beyond the most prosaic of his class.

And such, hitherto, he had in fact been ; but now, below the surface, lay a fiery impatience of the restrictions of his condition, and a resolute purpose to bend and mould all the circumstances of life to the achievement of Karslake's disgrace and Sybil's enfranchisement.

Therefore in order to attain this end he must renew the attempt to discover the hiding-place of the discarded mistress. It would be strange, with all his acuteness in fullest exercise, if Karslake should succeed in baffling him in the end.

CHAPTER XIX.

THE following six months were spent abroad by
the newly-married pair, Sybil seeing as much
of southern Europe as wealth, culture, and
devotion could procure.   They traversed Italy,
explored Switzerland and the Tyrol, wintered in
Rome ; they visited Greece, and returned slowly
home through Germany and France.   Their
experience of life during that time was as
of an enchanted cup held to their lips, brim full
of the essential wine of life.

To the one, to have only witnessed these
scenes of matchless interest, of glorious decay
and supreme physical beauty, would have been
a rapture of satisfaction had she been a poor

pilgrim on foot and unaided, ut doubtless
adventitious circumstances enhanced the charm.
If her husband's genius were less and his ardour
cooler than her own, his experience and culture
were greater; if she could quicken and fire
his intelligence by the inspiration of her spirit,
he in turn could guide and qualify the swift
conclusions of her intellect. If, beneath the
transcendant harmonies and soul-stirring bene-
dictions of the Christmas Eve services at St.
Peter's, or before the matchless statues and
bronzes of the Vatican, or some panorama of
snow-capped mountains kissed by the rising sun,
he retained his composure while her soul was
drunk with excess of passionate rapture, there
was no lack of generous and tender comprehension of her keener sensibilities. And then his
physical beauty, his sweet and gracious
manners (how sweet and gracious towards
herself!), and the fine chivalry of thought and

principle betrayed in conduct rather than in words, quickened and confirmed the coy and half-reluctant passion he had slowly excited in her mind. In perpetual contact with the seeming purity and simplicity of his nature, the remembrance of the incident that had so troubled their pre-nuptial peace almost faded from her mind, and the constant change, variety, and excitement of their nomad life prevented the touch of weariness or monotony.

But now the end of all this was drawing near. Karslake had stretched his furlough as far as his conscience would allow, and in spite of Sybil's undisguised reluctance decided upon going home.

'You forget,' he said smiling, ' that I have my work to do.'

' And will you be able to give me some work to do ? You must always remember I have lived a hard-working life, and shall never take

kindly to elegant idleness. I am not quite sure
I shall be able to adapt myself to a house like
yours, where there is nothing to mend or make,
to supplement or desire. I shall need to take
surreptitious lessons from my own servants. Do
you know I am half afraid I was not meant for
luxury and ease.'

'S. Mark's is a large parish,' he said ; ' there
are ten thousand human creatures in my so-
called cure. Don't you think a large-hearted,
gifted girl like you may find some employment
for your time amongst them ? '

' Possibly, but I doubt if I shall. If it were
a rural Dorset parish I could go in and out of
the cottages, teaching a woman here how to
make bread, washing and dressing a neglected
infant there, and talking to them all the time in
their own native dialect, but I am desperately
afraid of these Londoners ; their training,
notions, and aspirations are foreign to all my

experiences. And then, Julian, another point
it will be well for me to make plain at once.
I could not go to anyone in the character of
clergyman's wife—I mean in the sense of being
a teacher of religion. If they were in pain or
trouble I could feel with them, but I could not
talk to them about another world of which I
know nothing, or of God's plans, providences,
and requirements, about all which I am equally
in the dark. You look grave : you know it is
not I that have subscribed the Thirty-nine
Articles.'

'But you will go to church ? ' he asked.

'Yes, because it would be an act of dis-
courtesy towards my husband if I did not ; but
I think I shall ask you to accept it as a proof
of my wifely devotion. You know how I have
been brought up, how little I have been used
to Church-going, and, to be quite frank, I feel
no sense of deprivation in the past or of gain

in the present. Sometimes '—with a radiant smile—' if my mind is very weary, or again if it be very full, say, there is a new poem of Browning's to read or a novel of George Eliot's, I am afraid I shall beg you to let me off.'

'But you do not call yourself an unbeliever, Sybil ?'

'No. I stand, I think, just outside the pale of religious belief, listening to a voice that may one day speak to my inmost soul, but has not yet spoken. I am in suspense on all points of dogmatic teaching : God has only one aspect to me—the beneficent Creator of a world of magnificent possibilities of enjoyment, who has also endowed my own being with the capacity of tasting, perhaps of exhausting them. You may not think it, Julian, but mine has been a very happy life.'

'It must,' he answered, 'when you describe existence in such terms as these.'

There was a ring of pain in his voice that struck her with a feeling of surprise, but some finer instinct prevented her from expressing her comprehension of it, nor did she give any expression to the thought that rose in her mind that his experience had surely been a happy one too. She did not care to pursue the conversation, having already said enough to satisfy her conscientiousness, but it was a great relief to her mind that Karslake had neither deplored, protested, nor argued.

It was the absence of all ethical exigence on his part, his ungrudging readiness that all those about him should follow their own convictions, while never relaxing the strain of duty for himself, that made him one of the most lovable of comrades, the easiest of household companions. His unconscious unselfishness was a new and delightful study to a girl whose most intimate male connection had been of so different a type, and whose innate enthusiasm for moral excellence fed with healthy delight on these endearing manifestations. Her love for her husband deepened and broadened, leaving no room for the tameness and dissonance she had dreaded.

They had now got back to Bayswater and fallen into the routine of ordinary English life. The best members of a wide district and of several social circles, as followed from his profession, were anxious to become acquainted with them, and she was the most easily pleased and winning of youthful brides. She was prompt to recognise the smallest kindness and to be grateful for it, and her generous estimate of others and many-sided sympathies, not in the least narrowed by her intellectual bias, produced a natural charm and grace of manner which all pronounced irresistible. She could not only endure but disperse the tedium of the morning call, for in her intense vitality there was something that evoked and quickened that of her neighbour; and even the formal dinner-party had points of interest to one to whom as yet there was nothing flat, stale, or unprofitable in life.

In fact, she performed all the ordinary functions of high middle-class society, with a completeness and success which could scarcely have been expected from her character and training, or at least only by those who looked very far beneath the surface.

And at the same time and almost unknown to Karslake, she had made herself acquainted with some of the poorest and most miserable of his parishioners, and had so softened and won them by the freeness of her tender charity that she helped them one step nearer to the conception of the Divine. Karslake, too, soon learnt to discuss with her his plans of organisation and amelioration on all points of moral or

social reform, and to receive help and encouragement from the ardour of her sympathy and the
breadth and keenness of her intelligence.

Then there were the old home ties and
interests still in unbroken force : the boys had
spent half their long vacation at S. Mark's
Rectory, and Sybil had been proud and pleased
at their improvement both in mind and manners,
putting them through their scholarly paces with
unabated zest and capacity, and stimulating
their ambition by the greater ardour of her
own.

She went back with them to Ashlands for
a week's breath of Dorset air and the delight
of embracing her little ones and seeing for herself how things worked under the new régime—
the régime being a sensible middle-aged governess
for the children and an efficient help for
Hannah—and went back refreshed in spirit, and
with a deeper impulse of loving gratitude

towards the man to whom all this new comfort and brightness were owed.

In this even flow of tranquillity passed the first year of their marriage—no ominous event of the future casting its shadow before, and the only perceptible difference that time made in Mrs. Karslake's feelings was that, as the novelty and excitement of her new position subsided into custom and routine, the old literary and intellectual instincts stirred within her.

She had always been in the habit of concealing her authorship, and it scarcely glanced across her mind to break through a reserve she felt necessary for success by taking even her husband into her confidence. He was out as a rule for several consecutive hours in the day, and two or three of these Sybil devoted to her desk.

Her work was somewhat diversified She

had sent a translation of one or two fragments
of the ' Prometheus,' which had been graciously
received by a leading review ; she had reviewed
a popular novel in one of the weekly papers,
with a fine discrimination of judgment and
finish of style that had brought her a com-
plimentary invitation from the editor to work
on the staff; and, still more, she had published
an imaginative sketch in the shape of a short
story, in the pages of a Scotch magazine, which
by its united strength, delicacy and originality
was attracting general attention and setting
eager speculation on foot.

For all these things she was well paid, and
this fund she set aside untouched, animated by
the proud hope that by the time the boys were
ready for college, it might be of sufficient
amount to help considerably towards their
expenses.

For it must not be supposed that because

she had consented to the liberal arrangements made by Karslake, they ceased to be a burden to her pride and love of independence.

She was content personally to receive what he chose to bestow, but it still seemed distasteful to her that he should be the support of the family at large. Especially she felt the weight of obligation as regarded her brothers. Jack was earnestly bent on winning a scholarship at Winchester, to which she lent all the aid her sympathy could supply; should he succeed it might then be possible that both should run their University course without an application to her husband's purse.

The incentive was so powerful as to lend a more engrossing fascination to her labour than she had ever known before. She carried it on in her own charming morning-room before a writing-table at once adequate and elegant, and oddly in contrast with the old dilapidated desk of the Ashlands days. Karslake never came into this room without knocking for admission, nor she into his library, for he had a deep-rooted objection, he was wont to say, to the abolition of all courteous reserves in married intercourse. Sybil had none of the tendency to make a litter supposed to be common to a literary woman ; the neat manuscript she was engaged on was easily put out of sight in the few seconds before he entered, and he was not one of those men who invariably ask their wives ' what they have been doing ? '

Sometimes indeed there was a certain aspect, a faint carmine tint on the clear pale cheek, and a shining light in the dark eyes, that fixed his attention, but he never associated it with any unknown or concealed employment. He thought the pleasure of his coming had caused it, or perhaps the book she had been reading, for she was always surrounded by books, or the letter he had interrupted, had kindled her sensibility. And as his eyes dwelt upon her he also thought that she grew more beautiful and lovable every day, and he thanked God afresh for his felicity.

CHAPTER XX.

IT had been Gilbert Helstone's decision, after a
good deal of painful vacillation, to abstain from
using the permission he had been granted to
maintain his friendship with Mrs. Karslake.
His sense of decency prevented him from setting
foot in the house of the man he had so grossly,
if justly, insulted, and he entertained strong
doubts, which events seemed to justify, that
Sybil would care to renew their intercourse.

For all that his patience had been sorely tried
by the protracted absence of the married pair.
Now and again Sybil had written to Miss Helstone, and though these letters were chiefly of
a narrative or descriptive character, there were

slight incidental allusions to her companion that positively thrilled his disordered mind with jealous rage. How absolutely the man had fulfilled his own prophecy that he would make her love him!

It was a slight, though he felt unworthy, vent to his irritation to animadvert on the gross neglect of clerical duty which was involved in this half-year's abandonment of his parish, though Karslake had left an efficient substitute behind him, and to ridicule with the most scathing criticism every individuality of person, manner, or conduct. Some scarcely defined scruple of honour had prevented him from telling Sara in detail the scene he had witnessed at the Crystal Palace; he had contented himself with the assurance that when he condemned her model parson as liar and hypocrite, he spoke with sufficient cause, and sooner or later would prove his words.

Miss Helstone did not attach very much importance to these declarations; she looked upon her brother as a free-thinker who condemned as impostors all teachers of religion, and was also fully aware of the nature of his own feelings towards Sybil Dorrimore. All this made her tolerant but neglectful of his manifestations. This was so much the case that when they at length returned home Sara made the usual formal call with as little delay as possible, and brought back to her cynical companion the most enthusiastic account of the condition of things all round at S. Mark's Rectory.

'Did Karslake welcome you with effusion?' he asked. 'If you had taken the trouble to consult me I should have told you not to go.'

'I thought it likely, and avoided the collision. As for Mr. Karslake he never is effusive, and no doubt he resented your absence.'

'He would be quite prepared for that, Sara. My good girl, you must promise me not to go again.'

Helstone's voice as he spoke took its rarely tender tone; his sister looked at him anxiously.

'Not go again because of your unreasonable prejudices, Gilbert? Do you consider they are almost the only people I care to meet, and that I love the girl as if she were a younger and nobler sister?'

'Sybil must come and see us here,' he said in a low tone, and without looking at her; 'but you cannot visit at the house of a man of whom I entertain such an opinion as I do of Julian Karslake, and have moreover insulted to his face. I am very sorry, but it cannot be helped.'

He got up and left the room; his way of closing a discussion.

Sara sulked, rebelled a little, and finally

yielded, contenting herself with the mild
revenge of constant attendance upon the frequent services at S. Mark's, which she knew
tried her brother severely, though on this point
he did not interfere.

The constitutional perversity of her temper,
added to a conviction of the inexpediency of
bringing Mrs. Karslake into intercourse with
Gilbert, influenced her so far that she made no
attempt to induce Sybil to visit her for the first
few months after her return; but as time passed
on the desire to renew the old friendship and
confidence grew too strong for her objections,
and she wrote her a long explanatory letter,
which ended by entreating her to come and see
her sometimes, in spite of Helstone's unjust prejudices.

This letter Sybil having read and pondered
over, took to her husband. She went direct to
the library, believing him to be there, but

receiving no answer to her summons opened the door.

To her startled surprise she perceived that the room was not empty, as she had expected, but that Karslake was sitting before his writing-table with his head buried in his hands, in the attitude of a man lost in profound and painful rumination. She observed, too, in the first anxious survey that there was no evidence about him of any immediate employment— books and papers having been swept apparently on one side.

At the opening of the door, however, he looked up, but even when he saw who it was there was an absence of the usual brightening of expression.

He rose at once, and drew a chair for her nearer the fire.

'I need not say I did not hear you,' he said, and then he continued to stand opposite

to her, leaning against the high mantel with
his face somewhat averted, and again relapsed
into silence.

Sybil sat down in the seat indicated and
made some casual remark; that there was
something wrong in all the vague amplitude of
the phrase, she felt certain. His face was very
pale beyond its habitual lack of colour, and
there was a fixed contraction of the brows, and
a hardness altogether unknown to her observation before, in the lines of the mouth. Moreover, she perceived that his trouble or pre-occupation was so great that he found it difficult, or
perhaps impossible, to rally that power of self-
collectedness which so seldom deserted him.

It followed inevitably that her mind should
recur to the painful incidents which had preceded their marriage, and to which the slightest
allusion had never since been made, and that
the recollection should excite an involuntary

spasm of pain. Moreover, it made the task of introducing Sara's letter more difficult; her name would be a link of association with this hateful mystery.

To have asked him point-blank, as some women might have done, what was the matter, would have been impossible to Sybil's sensitive delicacy. She got up and went to his side : in that position he was not exposed to the embarrassment of her full gaze.

'I am afraid I have interrupted Sunday's sermon,' she said in her low vibrating voice, which seemed to give eloquence to her most careless words, 'for you have all the writer's look of preoccupation. I don't wonder you did not hear me, I knocked so softly.'

For answer he stooped down and kissed her hand, not with the tender passion of a lover or husband, but with an unmistakable movement of grateful thanks.

Then she looked up into his face and saw there an intensity of distress and pain greater than she had estimated at first, greater than it was possible for her love to ignore. As they stood thus side by side, her graceful head touched his shoulder; she turned round and clasping her slender hands about his neck looked earnestly into his face.

'Can I help you in any way, by speech or action I mean? If you can tell me what is the matter I am here to listen: otherwise you are free not to speak. I mean it will cause no soreness, no mistrust in my mind.'

He drew a breath of intense relief; his brow cleared and the usual expression of sweetness came back to his face. He bent towards her and kissed her sweet lips, but without the suggestion of strained feeling he had shown before.

'You have helped me already to the uttermost; there are few women capable of your magnanimity, Sybil: trust me, I will never prove unworthy of it.'

'I do trust you,' she answered in a low tone, and then there was a pause between them. He held her hand still clasped in his, but it was evident he was not going to confide in her, and she felt a sharp pang of cruel disappointment.

In her anxiety to conceal this fact she reverted somewhat abruptly to Sara's letter.

'I should like to read it to you,' she said. 'I do not quite know what answer to make.'

Having fulfilled her task and shown a great deal of unconscious zest and fellow-feeling with the writer in so doing, she looked anxiously towards Karslake, who had now recovered his usual equanimity, and had listened with quiet attention to the recital. He could not fail to see which way her wishes inclined, and the strong natural reluctance he had been on the point of expressing he decided to conceal.

'Go and see her, my darling, by all means—it will be an act of charity and friendship combined; and tell her what a warm sense I entertain of the old kindness she showed me. It is not my fault I do not call and thank her in person.'

'Is there no hope, Julian, of the misunderstanding between you and Gilbert Helstone being arranged? He was such a generous friend to us all when we had no other.'

'Sybil,' he answered with a grave smile, 'I scarcely think I shall find it possible for my wife to reconcile friendship for him with loyalty to me, though I am very sorry to say this. But if you think otherwise——'

'I own,' she replied eagerly, 'that the strength of my indignation against him has been greatly lessened by the experiences of the past year. He has not spoilt our happiness, he has forced it to a higher level. Is not my belief in you at this moment implicit, and what then does it matter that he tried and failed to shake it? Then I have so many dear memories connected with the old home, in all which he seems to have had a share, that I do not like to give him up; and very likely he has abandoned long before this the injurious suspicions he entertained at one time respecting you, Julian.'

Her voice fell and her colour rose a little as she spoke.

'No, he has not abandoned them,' replied Karslake quietly; 'but you are right in thinking his devotion to your family outweighs his enmity to me—from the virtue springs the vice. Do exactly as you wish, Sybil, not only in respect to Miss Helstone but her brother.'

The girl's beautiful face glowed and brightened; it was one of her strongest desires to see

Gilbert Helstone, and overwhelm his prejudice by proofs of her husband's merits.

'I will take you at your word, and go and see Miss Helstone after luncheon; and now '— more seriously—' I will leave you alone.'

She looked at him anxiously, half expecting and wholly hoping, he would seek to detain her, but he did not. He opened the door for her departure and closed it slowly after her, and then as slowly walked back to the seat he had occupied before she interrupted him, and bowed his face once more upon his hands.

He sat as motionless as if he had been turned to stone; there was no trembling of the strongly interlaced fingers, no groan or sigh to testify to the severity of the inward conflict. After a time he roused himself, and, taking two letters out of his pocket, prepared to re-read them, perhaps for the third or fourth time that morning.

The first was a daintily-tinted but ill-written note in a woman's handwriting, and ran thus:—

'I must see you to know what I am to do. My darling is dying and he is come back, and I am more than miserable.'

The other was a man's letter, and the writer was Gilbert Helstone. This was the wording of it:

'I am on your track at last and see my triumph close at hand. Take notice, I am better than my word, and give you the warning I refused.'

The bell rang for luncheon; Karslake refolded the letters, and rising wearily from his seat approached the hearth, and dropped them both into the glowing heart of the fire. He stood for a few moments watching them consume and trying to rally his courage and composure, and then as a test of his success went into the dining-room, and ate his luncheon in so much his accustomed manner that even Sybil's tender penetration was at fault.

As they rose from table she said :

' I am now going to Gilbert Helstone's, but I am not wilfully bent upon doing so. One lightest word from you, Julian, and I will give up the idea.'

He went up to her and kissed her with a grave tenderness.

' Go, by all means, my dear. If I should not be at home when you return do not wait dinner. I am obliged to go out on business.'

' On business,' she replied, ' beyond our late dinner-hour ! '

' Perhaps I ought to have said on duty. I am going to visit a sick child, and at a long distance from here.'

' So be it,' she answered ; ' then I can sit and gossip with Sara Helstone without compunction.' And so they parted.

CHAPTER XXI.

A SICK child—is there anything on earth more pathetic?—the heaviest burden and sorest penalty imposed on the infant pilgrim in the rough road of humanity.

It is nine o'clock at night and the late October rain is falling in torrents. In a small house in one of the most remote of the eastern suburbs, this common tragedy was being enacted. The child was lying in bed in an upper room simply or rather meagrely furnished; the disease was typhoid fever, but the stages of heat and frenzy had been passed, and he was now exhausted and comatose, and unconscious of all surroundings. The soft moulded limbs

have lost their roundness, and the face, touched
and marred by the foul fingers of disease,
much of its seraphic beauty, but to those who
knew him it would still not be difficult to
recognise him by the cloud of golden hair shed
over the pillow, the large-lidded eyes and
contour of delicate perfection.

A shaded lamp burns on a distant table and
throws heavy shadows around it. The neglected
fire in the untended grate is burning out to its
last embers, for the woman who is kneeling by
the bedside has lost all interest in external
comfort. She has knelt there hour after hour,
her elbows on the couch, her chin supported
on her hands and her distended gaze fixed
unweariedly on the boy. If you watch her you
will see how her whole being is absorbed in
her pitiful contemplation, for she reproduces as
if instinctively every slight movement on the
part of the child; her dress and appearance

show those signs of disorder and negligence
which suggest the idea of having watched day
and night—perhaps days and nights—by the sick
bed ; but weary and worn as she is she is still
very pretty, with a soft childlike loveliness that
possibly has gained interest and expression from
the intensity of her present suffering.

Mother and child are not the only occupants
of the room : on the further side of the bed,
almost beyond the range of light, a man is
seated in a comfortable American rocking-chair,
smoking a delicate cigar with apparent insensi-
bility, and with a tumbler of brandy and soda
conveniently placed on a small table at his
elbow.

It is curious to observe how entirely alien
and aloof the two groups appear from each
other ; her senses perceive nothing but the
child, his seem concentrated on the coarse
physical sensations of his employment. He is

so placed that the bed escapes the fumes of the
tobacco, and as he reclines at his ease lazily
watching the thin cloud he expels from his well
formed lips, it might be supposed he has no
interest or anxiety beyond.

But the conclusion would be wrong : in
his turn he has watched the child till his poor
powers of endurance are exhausted; she can
still kneel and agonise till the end; the strain of
the masculine mind must be relieved, and this
is the only relief that suggests itself to him.
Besides, it assists concentration of thought, and
he has a great deal to think of.

The silence is so profound, except as broken
by the heavy breathing of the boy, that the
sound of the door-bell, though evidently rung
by a guarded hand, startles them like an
electric shock.

Then the woman, who has turned perceptibly paler, looks across the bed at her companion.

'It is Julian,' she says in a low nervous
manner. 'I have sent for him. I did not
know what else to do.'

He sprang up from his seat with a coarse
oath upon his lips, flung his half-finished cigar
under the grate, and seemed to hesitate about
treating the contents of his glass in the same
way, but on second thoughts he changed his
mind and drained it to the bottom.

The next moment Julian Karslake entered
the room : he took in the scene at a glance—
the peril of the prostrate child, the despair of
the mother, the incongruous, defiant bearing of
the man.

For a moment the two stood on either side
of the bed gazing at each other, in height,
feature and general physique so singularly alike
that the most casual observer must have pronounced them brothers. But how much of
dissonance is compatible with likeness ! The one
looked as if the beauty of the inward nature

had moulded into affinity the outward aspect ; the other, as if the reckless and sensual soul was gradually degrading and blotting out the lines of physical perfection.

'Why are you here?' asked the elder sternly ; 'if your own promises do not bind you, have you lost sight of the risk you run?'

'I run!' repeated the other with a sneer, '*you* run rather! It is self-interest makes you so keen a watch-dog, good Julian, but there is a specific against misery even in misery itself. For my part I defy the law to condemn me to a more wretched life than I lead, while exposure to you would be as bad as the felon's dock or a cell at Millbank. Why am I here? Look at the poor little chap on the bed and answer that question for yourself.'

'The excuse would be sufficient—only you did not know he was ill.'

'Then, hang it, I came to see my girl, and,

by God, not even you shall come between us. Had it not been for this'—pointing to the bed —' you would not have caught me off my parole or she here. Your saved Magdalen was going back to her sins.'

'Is this true?' said Karslake, looking down at the kneeling figure at his feet. The girl winced and shrank beneath the compassion of his tone as if a blow had struck her.

'He has been here since yesterday,' she muttered, 'but I have scarcely looked at him or moved from Harry's side. I did not know he was coming nor why he came. I told you as soon as I could; what does it matter now? If Harry dies I shall have no heart to be good!'

Her voice rose in a wail of anguish; she suddenly flung her arms round Karslake's knees.

'Pray to God for me,' she sobbed, ' He will not listen to me. If you want to save me,

save him! Is Heaven so hard upon me
because I have no right to be a mother?'

In a moment the younger brother had cleared
the space between them, and tearing her from
her knees by an exercise of muscular strength,
he caught her in his arms and strained her
against his breast, soothing her and kissing her
wet cheeks with passionate abandonment.

'My poor Nell, my precious girl!' he said,
'has he brought you to this state of slavish
terror? God! if there be a God, who is dearer
to Him, think you—he in his prosperous, cold-
blooded formality, or you, sweet broken-hearted
darling? Come what may, my girl, we have
met and parted for the last time now.'

At first she had struggled to free herself
from his embrace, more from the sense of
Julian's presence than from any inward reluctance; but as the familiar tones and tender
caresses stirred the chords of old associations,

she grew passive and offered no further resistance. Her weary golden head, heavy with
pain and sorrow, rested on his breast with a
sense of habitude and languid pleasure; for a
few moments she forgot her child.

Karslake watched them both with sensations of mingled pain and sympathy, but he
abstained from interference till the first burst of
passionate feeling was over.

Then he went up to his brother and laid
his hand on his shoulder.

'Harry,' he said, 'there is but one way of
righting this wrong—will you do it?'

The other suddenly released his hold of
Nell, as if the suggestion unnerved him; he
looked up with his flushed face blanched with
fear.

'What do you mean? Have I not proved
to you again and again the thing is impossible,

absolutely more impossible than in the times gone by?'

'In the times gone by you based your objections on the plea that it would be below your social standing to marry the woman you had dishonoured; now you have lost that standing by an act of fraud that has, to my mind, not more of moral evil in it than much that you have done before, and through it all Nell continues to love you. Reward her fidelity by making her your wife, and she will not refuse to share your exile. Accept the one point of reparation in your power.'

'Accept my ruin! You mean I should marry her in my own name in the light of day? In other words you would give me up to justice, and so end the tax on your purse and your patience. You think you could face the world as a convict's brother? Not you! nor would Nell have much to thank me for if at this time of day, I made an honest woman of her in such a doubtful fashion. No, no, Julian, you salve your clerical conscience by offering a suggestion you know I shall refuse, and which otherwise you would never propose. It is scarcely worth while—we shall stick as close to each other as if your precious palaver had been spoken over our heads.'

'I am quite prepared,' replied Karslake quietly, ' to take my share of the risk and to smooth your way so far as it is in my power. You might meet at Bristol—it is easy to hide amongst the teeming masses of a sea-port town —and go straight from the church to the first vessel bound for the Antipodes. I will secure your berths and find all necessary funds.'

Harry burst into a coarse laugh. ' Are you, after all, in earnest in making such a proposal, or is it a trap to catch me unawares? Have you never heard of an extradition warrant?

What! my own name on the marriage licence and parish register! Shall I send my photo to Scotland Yard, and detail my dress, appearance and contingent whereabouts in the " Hue and Cry?" By God, Julian, parsons are the weakest fools on the face of the earth; for the sake of a contemptible social scruple to risk my liberty like that!'

'So weak a fool am I,' replied his brother, ' that I have reached the conclusion that the only right thing to do is to drop this miserable concealment, declare that you are still a living man, and take all the consequences of the confession. It may be the man you have wronged, or even the law itself, would deal leniently with you; but otherwise I would rather face life as a convict than live under such conditions as yours —and mine,' he added in a lower tone.

The other looked at him in speechless rage.

'You would betray me?' he asked in a suppressed choking voice, and making a menacing movement towards him.

'I shall never betray you, but if you decide to reject these terms you must at least keep those already made. You risk too much all round by coming here, besides destroying Nell's peace of mind. Also, except as your wife, she goes not with you. I will not ask you to go away to-night, while your boy is hanging between life and death, but you must leave this house; we will watch and let you know when the crisis is over. There is a little inn a stone's throw from here where you can sleep. I suppose you have some sort of disguise?'

Harry's lowering brow cleared a little.

'You mean straight and fair? You will not fail me? You have money with you?'

Karslake nodded assent; words were harder to produce.

Nell, meanwhile, had relapsed into her former mood, and was again kneeling beside the bed with her eyes fixed on the pallid, change-less face of the unconscious child. Julian went to the other side, and stooping over him took the tiny hand tenderly in his, in order to test the fluctuating feeble pulse, as well as to close a useless controversy.

Again at this moment the door-bell rang.

Nell looked up in alarm. 'It is the doctor! Harry, there is time to hide—that door leads into my dressing-room.'

Julian had turned quickly as the street-door was opened, and the voice of the childish maid-servant could be heard distinctly in parley with the visitor; he put gently down the frail hand he held, but his own shook perceptibly.

He had recognised the voice as Gilbert Helstone's. It was one of the crises of life; his own honour or his brother's safety hung in the balance.

One keen glance in Harry Karslake's face would have solved the mystery of the Crystal Palace, and wiped the infamous conclusions out. Two strides would have brought him within the shelter of the dressing-room, or otherwise he might have barred his brother's retreat; and the risk incurred by the latter was less than the certainty of his own injury and wrong.

But there was not the vacillation of a moment; to say the idea of self-preservation did not occur to his mind would be false, but it occurred only to be instantaneously rejected.

He stepped forward and opened the door behind him for Harry's hurried concealment, and closed it noiselessly again.

Then Nell spoke. 'You will not leave me! you will wait and hear what the doctor says? Or perhaps I ask too much?'

'It is not the doctor,' he said gently, 'or if it is, he is not alone. I recognise the voice of a man I know who has business with me and, I suppose, has followed me here.'

He hesitated, scarcely knowing what step to take or suggest. Was he tamely to submit to the insufferable outrage of Helstone's espionage? And yet of what avail would protest or controversy be when his lips were sealed to silence, even had such resource been possible under existing circumstances.

It was now evident from the sound of voices below that Helstone was not alone—he had probably entered the house with the doctor, who was questioning the servant-girl as to whether he should go up to the sick room at once. Nell sprang to the head of the stairs and begged him to do so, and the next moment both he and the stranger entered the room together.

So great was the poor mother's pre-occupation that she scarcely heeded the intrusion, or
accepted Julian's explanation as sufficient ; he
on his part raised his eyes and met Helstone's in-
solent, defiant glance with dauntless equanimity.
There was no opportunity for the exchange of
words ; Karslake was standing on the further
side of the bed, which the doctor had immediately approached in order to examine his
patient ; Nell awaiting his fiat with her eager
gaze fixed on his face, and her whole soul in
her gaze. But the mind of the professional
man himself was alert and open ; though his
first keen glance was at the child his next was
at the stranger, whose striking personality
challenged attention. It was the first time in
his visits to mother and son that he had seen
any man about the house, and his curiosity had
been considerably excited as to the status of his
clients ; the rapid conclusion he now reached as

his eyes searched Karslake's face, was a very
satisfactory one to the doubts he had entertained.

'Your husband, I presume, my dear
madam?' he said, acknowledging Karslake's
courteous recognition of his approach.

Poor Nell's face and neck were dyed crimson with complex confusion and shame; she
cast an agonised glance of deprecation towards
Julian, to whose pale cheek also the colour
slowly rose. He knew Helstone's cruel cynical
eyes were watching every manifestation, and
translating each into damning evidence against
him.

For all that neither gesture nor voice
betrayed the slightest agitation. He replied
quietly :

'You are mistaken, but none the less I am
deeply interested in your patient. What do
you think of him? I have thought his sleep

more natural during the last quarter of an hour, and there is a little moisture on the skin.'

The doctor shrugged his shoulders almost imperceptibly; he concluded he understood the situation perfectly, and was a little revolted by the coolness of the speaker : besides, he resented instinctively any unprofessional opinion of the case. He began feeling the child's pulse, testing the temperature, and then raised the heavy lids and peered into the dilated pupils beneath. At the end of his investigation he shook his head ominously.

'Surely you find some hopeful symptoms?' urged Karslake in the same tone of anxiety as before, and trying to direct the doctor's attention to the white face of the stricken mother at his side; 'I have seen patients rally from a state of coma as profound as this, and begin to revive.'

'It is possible—just possible,' was the reply, 'but the boy appears to me to have been a little neglected ; to be sure, my dear madam, you could not know what to do in these changed conditions. Everything now depends on the nursing he gets ; he must be watched hour by hour, and every symptom observed and provided for. Tired eyes and weary limbs won't do—you must go to bed and find some one else to sit up ;' he looked at Karslake a little maliciously. 'His lips must be moistened continually with wine and water or milk, if you have got any. I will send a draught that must be administered in case of returning conscious-ness—that is, if he is able to swallow.'

Then Helstone spoke from the remote cor-ner of the room, where he had been standing a silent spectator of the scene.

'It will, no doubt, be a great disappoint-ment to Mr. Karslake that his engagements will make it impossible for him to spend the night with the child, in spite of his natural desire to do so.'

The unfamiliar name fell flat on the doctor's ear, and he made no sign. It could not be otherwise than that Julian understood the animus of the speaker, but no change of expression bore witness to the fact.

'It will be inconvenient for me to sit up all night,' he said, addressing the doctor, 'but not impossible. It is necessary that the mother should rest, and there is no one else to take her place. But in that case I must find a messenger to deliver a note at my own house.'

'I am going home immediately,' said Helstone, 'and must of necessity pass your door. I will deliver a letter if you think me sufficiently trustworthy.'

There was a ring of almost diabolic triumph in his voice, and for the first time Karslake turned and looked at him with an expression that indicated something of the moral recoil he excited. He did not however refuse the offer.

'If you will come down-stairs into another room we can perhaps arrange it:' and then he turned to Nell to make some inquiries about writing materials, speaking to her in his usual tone of gentle consideration, to which his present sympathy gave an added touch of tenderness and respect.

She, poor soul, to whom he had always appeared as an angel of God, looked up to him with eyes so full of passionate feeling that Helstone might well be excused for thinking the last point of confirmation had been added to his conclusions. He preceded Karslake down-stairs, with such a tempest of rage and hatred in his heart that he half doubted his power to hold it within decent control.

Here was evidence sufficient for the Divorce

Court—evidence that must rouse the meekest and most credulous of wives into relentless revolt. Sybil, the barely year-old wife, already wearied of and betrayed, while the husband returned to his earlier and baser passion.

He had not himself expected anything so bad as this; he had indeed firmly believed in the guilt and dishonour of the past, but had supposed that marriage would have put an end to it. Even the easy morals of society would have exacted this as an indispensable point of decency, but the effrontery of the priest's transgression mocked at even conventional limits. Then his mind dwelt on his own strong love for the wronged and outraged girl; how the lightest touch of her hand on his, still more the tender kiss of friendship she had sometimes given in the sweet past, made every pulse in his being thrill with the agony of vain desire. She had given herself body and soul to this man,

with the most insane but generous confidence
—and this was her reward!

And—the pity of it! the pity of it!—not
two hours before he had seen her dear face
kindle, and tender voice take a sweeter inflection, as she described and eulogised the daily life
and character of the husband who was at that
very moment renewing his vows to his mistress
and soothing her maternal grief.

The little parlour down-stairs had no fire, and
was only lighted by the candle Karslake had
brought down in his hand. He placed it on a
table, found pen and ink as if familiar with the
arrangements of the place, and sat down to
write his letter without word or look towards
his companion.

Helstone had closed the door and stood
glaring at him with his back against it. It
was not his intention, if he had sufficient
restraint over himself, to vent his wrath and

disgust in speech : he could afford to wait now that he saw his way to his perfect revenge. He watched him as he wrote with venomous intensity: as the sickly ray of the candle fell direct on his enemy's face he saw with a thrill of triumph its extreme pallor, and that the hand that dipped the pen into the ink shook perceptibly. He could hardly refrain from tearing the paper from under his fingers, and refusing to be the medium of conveying his words of falsehood and cajolery to the unhappy and deceived wife at home: only his success would be all the more complete if he could abstain from violence or threatening now. Some slight contemptuous surprise he felt at Karslake's invincible firmness and composure under the knowledge of his own complete exposure, of the scathing reprobation excited and the consequences that must ensue. But that reserve of outward manifestation was one of his most

baffling characteristics; and it was precisely
to such consummate aptitude for deception that
Sybil owed her ruin and his hate its keenest edge.

The note was brief and penned rapidly after
the first pause of deliberation; then Karslake
sealed the envelope in which he had placed it
and rose from the table.

'Before putting this letter in your hands,'
he said, 'you will not think it unreasonable that
I ask for an assurance that you will simply
deliver it at the door. I mean that you will
make no attempt to see Mrs. Karslake.'

'I shall make no attempt to see Mrs.
Karslake to-night. It would be too late. My
compact goes no farther.'

'In that case I will light you to the door.
I am anxious to return to the sick-room, and I
imagine your object is gained.'

'Aye, beyond my most sanguine expecta-
tion! But I will dispense with ceremony. I

prefer to let myself out with my own hand. You will scarcely expect me to say good-night— there is not a curse in the repertory of the blasphemer that I would not rather invoke on your head.'

And with these words he opened the door, groped his way along the dark passage, and let himself out into the still falling rain.

Karslake stood for a few moments after he had heard the door close behind him, poured out and drank a glass of water from a bottle that stood on the table near him, and then slowly took his way upstairs again.

CHAPTER XXII.

THE first thing Karslake did on returning to the room, after the departure of the doctor, was to organise arrangements for the night, and make some change in the pillows and position of the still unconscious child, for Nell, though a devoted mother, was a bad nurse. Then he dismissed the exhausted girl to bed, advising her to take the servant into her apartment with her for further precaution.

'I will see Harry safely off the premises,' he said, 'and you may depend upon my calling you if any change for the worse should occur in the child.'

'But the doctor's boy has not brought the

medicine yet,' she answered fretfully ; ' the maid or I must sit up for that.'

' There is no need. I will open the door myself and then shut up the house.' Seeing she still hesitated, he added :

' Are you afraid I shall not understand the directions on the bottle ? '

' O no, not that ; but lest you should do yourself still more harm.'

' That will not follow,' he said kindly. He did not add, ' because all the harm possible has been already done,' though that was his inward comment. ' Try and dismiss all your anxieties and sleep soundly, so as to be fit for the work of to-morrow. I hope and believe he will rally, but he will need a good deal of patient nursing, and you must not wear out your strength.'

She went at last, and then, after having surveyed his little patient and wetted the parched lips according to instruction, he opened the door of the inner room, where his brother lay concealed, and went in.

There was a couch in one corner of the apartment, and on this Harry Karslake had flung himself, and was at the moment lying fast asleep. The light from the adjoining room was just enough to reveal the attitude of careless ease, the quiet, untroubled slumber he was enjoying, and, as is often the case, his face under this aspect seemed to have recovered much of the innocent repose of youth.

The elder brother leaned against the wall and looked down upon him ; then, moved by that instinct of protection which had always marked their relations, he took up a woollen shawl that was thrown over the back of the sofa and spread it over him. Light as the touch was it was sufficient to awake him ; he sprang up with an anxious and aggressive air.

'Oh, is it you, old fellow?' he said testily.

'Come to tell me it is time to be moving? A hunted man sleeps like a hare. Hang it, Julian, there are days and hours when I am half disposed to take your advice, throw up the sponge, and give in. Five years of pious propriety would see me out of Dartmoor with a ticket-of-leave; then Nell and I could be spliced without further bother, if she had proved faithful, and we would hide our disgrace in one of the cities of Australia. If the little chap lives he should go with us—what do you say?'

'As I have said before; that it is the only way back to peace and honour, if you have courage enough to pay the penalty.'

The words were spoken almost mechanically, and the other looked in his face and uttered a low mocking laugh.

'I am scarcely the dupe you take me for,' he said; 'if you really thought I spoke in good faith your shame and terror would be tenfold

mine.   You would urge me *for our mother's sake*
to save the name you bear from public disgrace,
and double your bribes for my expatriation.
Own it!   You have married lately—was that
an honourable thing to do?'

'It would have been a dastardly thing to do
if I had known you were alive and a criminal
when I first sought to win my wife.   I learnt
the former fact from Nell Trevelyan a month
before my marriage, and the latter not till my
return from my wedding tour.   From that hour
to this I have incessantly revolved in my mind
the right course to pursue.   I am pledged at
all points not to betray you; but decide to surrender yourself to justice, and you may count
upon me to back you at all costs.'

'To stand in the dock at my side at the
Central Crim.,' sneered Harry, 'and subse-
quently to face your church and fine wife in
the new character of convict's brother?   You,

whose whole life—come, I'll allow that much —has been given to the pursuit of whatsoever things are lovely and of good report, to be flung so deep into the mire? No, no, Julian; you are a very good fellow in your little way, but take my word for it, you are not quite tough enough for that.'

'Try me!' was the almost passionate answer. 'Give me leave to go to Mr. Anstruther and tell him you are the one survivor of the wrecked fishing-smack in which you made your escape, and that you choose to stand the penalty of a half-involuntary crime rather than to spend life in vagabondage and exile. It is possible that time has softened his enmity: I would offer him restitution to the farthest claim of principal and interest, and if not——'

'Aye, there comes the pinch! I own my heart leaps at the chance of being a free man once more. How I curse the moment when I

was fool enough to add that little nought to
his niggardly cheque—seems to me now that
the incarnate devil himself would not tempt me
to such idiot folly again. A stroke of the pen
—the impulse of half a moment—to wreck a
man's whole life! But I know Mr. Anstruther;
there is the venom of the Scotch trader in his
blood, and he has hated me like poison from a
child. No, Julian, no; I'll not risk it: nothing
would induce him to forego his pound of flesh.
They might give me twenty years.'

Karslake was silent.

'I must be off,' resumed the other. 'I shall
find my way down to the docks in the morning,
and book myself as an A.B. in the first ship
chartered for the Antipodes. So I found my
way home—even Nell's faithful memory did
not penetrate my disguise at first. I suppose,
cowed by your croaking, there is small chance
of her joining me, should I send for her in time

to come?   And now to business : are you prepared to bleed freely?'

'I have two hundred pounds with me ; when
you reach your destination write, and if possible
I will arrange the transmission of periodical
sums.   But you will work?'

'As an alternative to starving I will work, not
otherwise; but what you propose can't be done.
Fate makes me a vagabond ; but I will let you
know, depend upon it, when and how money can
reach me.'

He took and secured the leathern purse
his brother held out to him, and then stooped
and lifted a heavy carpet-bag that was pushed
out of sight under the couch.

'This is my toggery of transfiguration,' he
said, with forced gaiety ; 'but I will put it on
down-stairs before the little glass in the parlour.
I would rather you did not see me in it : at
some future time it might put your truth-speak-

ing to an awkward test. You will bid her good-bye for me ?'

'I will, but wait a moment! It is almost more than I can bear to see you relegate yourself to a life of hardship and wretchedness; is there no other alternative possible?'

'None; as a man sows, &c. The parting is a pinch—to you—but you will soon get over it. And, to help to harden your heart, remember the life I led you in the days of old; how I ridiculed your affection, mocked your advice, and aggravated my sins out of very wantonness, to give you pain. Look at the sequel as the whipping I have richly deserved, and—good-bye.'

'What I remember,' said Karslake retaining his hand in an almost painful grasp, 'is the innocent curly-headed child who lay sobbing in our dying mother's arms, and the promise she extracted from me then—" to strive for your welfare at any personal cost." How miserably have I failed in its fulfilment!'

'Not entirely your own fault, my good Julian! My bias unfortunately seems to have been the same as the Psalmist's—"I went astray from the wcmb speaking lies." I don't think I was ever an innocent child; I told fibs, and prigged the sugar and jam long before the period you mention, though the dear guileless creature never suspected it. And for a while I hoodwinked my big brother too. But it is time to have done with these reminiscences —only you have recalled the old pledge given on a death-bed—you will never forget it?'

'So far as the memory of it can help you, I will never forget it.'

'You are very fond of your wife, Nell tells me; also that she is wonderfully pretty. There are moments of conjugal lapse and softness when a man lets his very soul leak out its secrets.

You will be on your guard against such? You will never own your brother is a living man?—renew your promise!'

'I promise.'

'"At any personal cost," the dear mother said,' continued the younger man bitterly, 'and I have cost you something already. None the less, you have all the good things of life in possession, and the darling is the outcast! There is precious little you can do for me now. Still my mind would be easier if you would clinch your naked promise with an oath.'

'My word binds me for life or death,' answered Julian, 'you need no other security.' Then looking again into the sullen, dissatisfied face of the other, he added, 'As you will; dictate what words you please, short of impiety, and I will repeat them after you.'

A twinge of compunction pierced the

callous sensibilities of Harry Karslake as he encountered his brother's glance.

'Let it pass!' he said impatiently; 'you would cavil at my prescription for certain. Only remember, I hold you bound in tighter bonds than if you had called down hell and damnation upon your head.'

He turned abruptly from him, and going into the other room stood for a moment by the bed and looked at the child.

Julian followed him, full of anxiety for his involuntary neglect, but there was no change to be perceived.

'I wonder if this youngster and I will ever see each other again!' muttered Harry. 'Not much matter if we don't. Mind, I leave him to you as my representative of virtue and honour —make a better man of him than his father! I would kiss him but he smells of fever. No more farewells—I'm off—don't follow me!'

He went down-stairs, and Julian heard him shut and lock the parlour door upon himself; in less than ten minutes' time it was reopened, and the wanderer let himself out into the darkness of night.

CHAPTER XXIII.

It was ten o'clock in the morning of the following day. Mrs. Karslake, who retained her country taste for early rising, had already breakfasted and dismissed her light household duties. The persistent rain was still falling so that she could not go out; her husband had not yet returned, and this would give her a longer spell of leisure than usual over her beloved manuscript.

She went into her morning room, where a bright fire gave the effect of homely comfort to enhance its dainty luxury and ease. For a few moments she moved about among her cabinets, her soft gray dress and light footfall

making no sound, taking up with a tender wist-
ful air some of the costly trifles with which
they were strewn. As she thus handled and
examined the perfect bronze, the priceless bit of
old china, the thought that passed through her
mind was how soon she had familiarised herself
to this new atmosphere of lavish expenditure,
this indulgence of æsthetic instincts ; and how
the value of one of these artistic toys would
have seemed a mine of wealth to her but a short
year ago.

She had known so much of the pressure of
poverty that she was half doubtful of the right
of spending so much on the externals of life, and
like all beings of deep feeling and high aspira-
tion, was inclined to ask herself what right she
had to a happiness so exceptional as her own.

She had her husband's note in the pocket of
her dress, and she drew it out and read it over
again. All she knew was that it had been left

by a messenger at the door the previous evening, and she did not read it again from any
sense of dissatisfaction with its contents, for her
loyal and unsuspicious nature accepted the explanation of his absence as thoroughly adequate.

Her motive was to see if she had missed
any intimation of the time she might expect
his return that day.

She still held it in her hand when a servant
entered with a card.

'Was she at home to so early a visitor?'

The card bore Helstone's name, and Sybil
turned a little pale as she read it, some subtle
impression touching her that there was a connection between this unusual visit and Karslake.
Had it not been for this indefinable suspicion
she would have felt a girlish pride in receiving
her old friend in her new home.

'Yes,' she said, 'I am at home and will see
Mr. Helstone at once.'

When the door opened she crossed the room to meet him, but started back involuntarily at the sight of his pale and haggard countenance.

'What is wrong?' she asked eagerly. 'Has something dreadful happened at your own house?'

Helstone looked her through and through with his keen hungry eyes : he had spent not only a sleepless night, but had made no attempt to court sleep, counting the slow hours till the time when he could decently call upon the woman he loved and pitied beyond measure, in order to fulfil his stern duty towards her, and inflaming both his love and his hate during the protracted vigil.

And now he saw her for the first time with all her luxurious surroundings, happy and smiling in perfect ignorance of the blow with which he was to destroy her peace. There was no anxiety in that clear glance, or shadow of conjugal suspicion in tone or aspect. For a moment he hesitated. Had it been a question of pure self-sacrifice he had been equal to make it, but it behoved him as a point of relentless duty to open her eyes to her own dishonour; his heart would bleed for her, but he had told her husband that when the hour arrived for her enlightenment, he would choose misery for her rather than disgrace.

'My dear,' he said, taking her hand quietly, 'it is not in my own house that something dreadful has happened, and you may be quite sure I should not cross the threshold of yours except under some form of compulsion.'

There was a deliberate solemnity in his manner that could not but produce its effect. It was unlike the vindictive prepossession he had revealed on other occasions when her husband was the subject of his warnings and reproach;

she could not help recalling, with a pang, the
agitation she had witnessed the day before, and
dreading lest some inevitable connection was to
be traced between it and Karslake's singular and
unexpected absence.   For all that, the courage
and loyalty of her nature moved her to repress
the slightest sign of misgiving.

'Sit down,' she said, drawing a chair
towards the fire and taking another herself,
opposite to him; 'it is such a pleasure to me to
see you at last in my own house that I will
not inquire too closely into the motive of your
coming.   I am quite sure it is out of regard to
what you think my true interests.'

'Think!' he repeated, with a sort of
pathetic bitterness; and then he took the chair
offered, and sat for a moment or two gazing
into the sweet serene face with a feeling of
remorseful tenderness.

'I am risking all I care for most in coming

here to-day,' he resumed. 'Whether you believe or pretend to disbelieve the truth of what I am going to tell you, you will equally hate me for the telling of it. You got the note I brought last night?'

'*You* brought!'

'Yes; strange as it may well appear that I should play lackey to Mr. Karslake. But I spared you a night of watching and anxiety— that was my actuating motive. He is not come home?'

'Not yet,' she answered, with a tender dignity that touched him to the quick. 'I do not expect him yet.'

'It may be,' he rejoined passionately, 'that even his audacity is scarcely equal to facing immediately the wife he has outraged. Nay, Sybil, command your patience a few moments,' for she had made a gesture of indignant repudiation—'you must listen to what I have to say.'

'But I refuse to listen! It was incumbent upon me to do so once, as a guest in your house and before any legal ties bound me to Julian Karslake. Now I am his wife, and even you shall not malign him in my presence.'

'Malign!' he repeated, almost maddened by her expression of proud confidence and the fear of defeat, and pouring out his words in defiance of her protest, 'do I malign him by the statement of plain facts? I saw him last night leaning over the bedside of his dying child, and admitting to the very doctor in attendance that the tie that bound him to its mother was an illicit one. It was to console that unhappy mother that he absented himself from home last night.'

Sybil had tried and failed to arrest the words, and now that she had heard them it was as much as she could do to repress the cry of anguish they seemed to tear from her heart. She got up from her seat pale as death, but still maintaining her proud and resolute demeanour. Her first impulse, doubting her own strength, had been to lean against the mantel-piece for support, but she checked it as an indication of weakness.

She felt like some stout swimmer from whose grasp the saving rope has been torn, but who still relies on his own ability to regain it. For a brief space, while those cruel words were in her ears, she felt her hold upon her husband's honour slackening, and it was a space that seemed to enclose within it the very bitterness of death; but already her faith revived. It had only been a momentary and instinctive disloyalty.

Helstone, intensely observant of the effect of his words, had made a movement of eager sympathy towards her, but she repelled him with an imperious gesture. He misunderstood her entirely.

'Sybil,' he murmured, devouring the pathos of her face with his burning gaze, 'when the first shock of outraged womanhood is past, you will learn to thank me for putting it in your power to prove your right to freedom. Never, surely, was so sweet a woman so sinned against before!'

'Is it possible,' she asked, with a brave and successful effort to speak calmly, 'that you believe that I have accepted your assertions? My trust in Julian's fidelity at this moment is as absolute as if you had never spoken. What grieves me is the determined malice and cruelty of one who has been my friend until to-day. Henceforth, Mr. Helstone, you and I are strangers.'

He stared at her for a moment in incredulous astonishment, then broke into a derisive laugh.

'Child,' he said, 'what good will it do to

play off these queenly airs on me? Will your
infatuated refusal to believe in facts rob these
facts of their remorseless stubbornness? All
these circumstances, which a happy chance has
brought under my own cognisance, I shall lay
before the next meeting of Mr. Karslake's
parish. As a parishioner I have a right to
do this, though even as an outsider I should be
justified in exposing such a nefarious imposture as his. I can produce witnesses in support
of my accusations. Shall you be content to
wait and see how he rebuts the charge?'

She looked at him with a sort of confused
horror. His relentless face, the cruel tones of
his voice, seemed to obliterate the individuality
of the kind and genial man she had known in
former years, and the threat he now uttered
was a formidable one. Would he do this thing?
She saw at a glance it involved ruin to her
husband; for granting that he consented to

repudiate the accusation, no reputation is fair enough nor virtue sufficiently pure to resist the tarnish of so foul a suspicion. And if, as she knew was possible, he should refuse to consent?

'You cannot mean what you say,' she answered at last, passing her hand over her brow with an irresistible movement of oppression; 'it would be an act of absolute malignity. Why do you make so sure of his guilt? I should have thought your professional knowledge of life might have taught you how often appearances and truth are at variance. Cannot you conceive of circumstances that may bind the lips of an innocent man to silence?'

'An innocent man! By God, Sybil, you try me more than I can bear! An innocent man, whom I have seen with his doting mistress at his knees, and his false face white with anxiety for the bastard he denies! You, blind with conjugal passion, believe I am going to throw dirt on the white raiment of a saint. Instead, I am going to discover the vilest hypocrite that ever walked.'

'You think so. I know you conscientiously think so, but you are wrong.' She spoke in a voice of passionate though controlled emotion, but it only served to intensify his sense of her incredible delusion.

'You plead in vain,' he said sternly, 'for it is my zeal for your own honour and happiness that moves me in this matter. It is just possible that I may have an alternative to propose hereafter, but that will need further consideration.'

There was a pause between them, during which Sybil's ears caught the sound of the door-bell and the slight bustle of an arrival. The next moment she heard Karslake's voice inquiring of the servant where she was. She rose immediately.

'My husband is come,' she said, 'and I must go and meet him. I will return and speak to you again, if you think fit to wait;' and then she crossed the room swiftly, 'on the wings of her insensate love,' he thought to himself, and went out, closing the door upon him.

The next moment she had joined Karslake in the hall, where he still stood somewhat slowly and wearily divesting himself of his overcoat; and drew him with a gracious smile and touch into the library, which was the room nearest at hand.

'Come here, and let me look at you,' she said, with an assumption of rare playfulness. 'I want to see how you bear the brunt of a night's watching.'

She was standing in the embrasure of the bay-window, but the dismal October day shed but a murky light. He went close up to her, put his hands lightly on her shoulders, and

looked down into her upraised face. Their
eyes met with intense though restrained expression. He looked not only pale and weary,
which fatigue might easily have justified, but
absolutely wan and haggard, but for all that
the gaze that met hers was as clear and steadfast as ever.

'Have you some questions to ask, some
misgiving to satisfy? You look at me, Sybil,
as if you wished to question not my face, but
my heart and soul. Are you displeased?'

'Is the child better?' was her answer.

In point of fact she had probed as deep as
he suggested, and was fully satisfied with the
result, but some subtlety of feeling induced her
to play on the verge of the escaped danger.

'He is conscious this morning, but I fear
will scarcely have strength to rally.'

'And that will be a great grief to you?'

'It will be a great grief to me,' he answered

gravely, 'and almost a death-blow to his unhappy mother.'

In spite of her firmness, Sybil involuntarily
drew back a little and changed colour. Then,
as she met his questioning and almost stern
glance, the crimson rushed into her face; it
was she who dropped her eyes as if conscience-
stricken.

'Can it be possible,' he said, 'that you have
seen Gilbert Helstone?'

'He is in the house at this moment. I
have only just left his presence to give you a
welcome home.'

Karslake turned pale even to the lips; his
eyes kindled and scintillated with passion.

'This is an outrage that cannot be suffered,'
he said hoarsely, and crossed the room to lay
his hand on the bell.

Sybil sprang forward to arrest the movement.

'What are you going to do, Julian?
Summon some servant to dismiss him and exasperate him still further? No, no; I want you to
take another course from that!'

He forbore in deference to her entreaty, but
at the same time he turned from her with a
haughty coldness that cut her to the heart.

'You said just now you came to welcome
me home. What am I to think, Sybil,—that
you are able to reconcile your duty to me with
Gilbert Helstone's intolerable persecution?
Have you allowed him to tell you what happened
last night?'

'I have allowed it,' she answered, with a
sense of injustice that brought tears of agonised
disappointment to her eyes, 'simply because
it was physically impossible to prevent it.
What more could you require than that I
should protest against his calumnies before they
were uttered, and indignantly repudiate them

afterwards? Do you count it nothing that in face of the evidence he puts forward, I still retain my faith in your fidelity?'

'That is,' he said, in a low suppressed voice of concentrated indignation, 'that I am to be grateful because you, my wife, hesitate to believe me guilty of an almost incalculable depth of baseness and treachery,—that the perjured lover of last year is the shameless adulterer of to-day? You imply that the evidence is so strong to that effect, that you go beyond reason and claim the dues of magnanimity in not accepting it? And I, on my part, say——' and then he stopped abruptly. 'I am not equal to this contention to-day,' he added, more calmly, 'and the less I say the better. I will accept the faith you still retain, Sybil, and try and be thankful that you are disposed to welcome me home.'

He stooped and kissed her as he spoke, as

if he remembered this conventional act of greeting had not passed between them, and then turned and left the room.

Sybil drew a breath of intense mental pain, but it was for him not for herself. The measure of passionate feeling which he had manifested had shown her, as he had never done before, what was the extent of suffering produced by the false position in which he was placed, and excited her minutest comprehension and tenderest sympathy.

He was right in resenting her appeal to his consideration. To believe in him was indeed the most elementary of duties, and his own acute sense of outraged rectitude might well render him sensitive to doubt or hesitancy on her part. Never should he accuse her of such laxity again !

She sat down in his accustomed seat, and covering her face with her hands, tried to con-

centrate her mind upon the situation. This
state of things could not continue; and she was
unable to deny that the position was not only
inexplicable, but to the cool eye of reason incredible as well. Granting that their conjugal
happiness could stand this desperate strain, what
motive was adequate enough to justify her
husband's exaction of it? She was certain of his
love for her: what then must be the power of
this terrible influence which could neutralise
so many and supreme obligations?

At this point she recalled Helstone's
recent threat with a feeling of abhorrence that
was increased by reflection, but at the same
time with some dawning sensation of relief.
The remedy was, indeed, nauseous and desperate, but it might succeed in effecting the result
desired. It was morally impossible to suppose
that Karslake would sacrifice his public
character and credit, and cut short a useful and

exemplary career by persistence in this obstinate silence. The spiritual martyrdom of such a course of action would be so terrible to a man of his temperament, that the prospect of it would surely suffice to shake his resolution.

At this moment she heard and recognised Helstone's step in the passage; he was doubtless tired of waiting for her return, and on the point of departure. She rose and went out into the hall to meet him, for though she would have disdained to propitiate him on her own account, she stifled any such reluctance where her husband's interests were concerned.

'I was coming back to speak to you,' she said. 'Have you anything more to say to me?'

'Only to bid you ponder what I have told you this morning, and to convey to Julian Karslake my intentions as regards the future. Ah! that touches you, Sybil, but I have no pity! Rather, mine is a sort of heavenly discipline. I will not

spare a single stroke of the rod that may serve
to break your infamous union.'

'And how would that do it?' she asked,
with a smile of quiet contempt.

'How? If he should continue to refuse to
tell you the truth under the pressure I am going
to put upon him, even you can no longer affect
to doubt his guilt; and that admitted, Griselda
herself would refuse to live with him. A wife
that could condone such offences would sink to
the level of the man's degradation, or below it.
You think me hard? I am, and nothing could
have made me so, short of infamy like his and
infatuation like yours. But there is your
luncheon-bell. I will wish you a better appetite for your repasts than I have had for mine
lately.'

CHAPTER XXIV.

WHEN husband and wife met again there was no reference made to the painful incidents of the last twenty-four hours. Karslake had recovered his usual composure, and Sybil perceived by his manner that he strictly guarded himself against inquiry or explanation. She said to herself, 'he does not fail to take me at my word, and stretch "my inflexible belief" to the uttermost.'

But as her loving faith responded to the demand, she felt no sense of injury; only in the near future it would behove her to enter again on this controversy, and demonstrate to him that silence and secrecy could be maintained no longer. For the present each took up their respective interests and duties with the same zeal, to all appearance, as before.

Perhaps, as regards Karslake, it was in fact the same, as his conduct was dictated by principles beyond transient and external influences ; or it might even have been that the ceaseless watchfulness necessary against self-betrayal, the added strain upon his moral nature, led to a more thorough and determined devotion.

At least so it seemed to the tender and penetrating eyes that watched his daily performance of his routine duty, with unhalting interest and approval. She had known him at times, and cordially excused it, a little impatient with the incessant claims upon his time and energy naturally occurring in a parish like S. Mark's, where the rector was known to identify himself with the life and welfare of all classes of his parishioners ; but now his readiness to meet

every demand was unfailing in its quiet promp-
titude.

Nor did this additional stringency assume a
harsh or ostentatious character, or lead him to
neglect or curtail any of the social or intellectual indulgences in which she took delight. To
her his manner had the same tender suavity as
before ; a little less caressing and light-hearted
perhaps, but still more earnest and solicitous.
Wherever she went amongst the poor she heard
his praises spoken, and discovered that scarcely
one-half of his self-denying labours in their
behalf came under her own observation or
knowledge.

But, in spite of all this outward calm, Mrs.
Karslake owned to herself that her blessedness
was a thing of the past. To watch the rigorous
performance of duty in the man she loved,
under conditions of harassing personal anxiety,
no allusion to which he ever allowed to escape

his self-control, might exalt the passionate esteem in which she held him, but, at the same time, it was a laying of the axe to the root of her peace of mind. There was none of the happy freedom from care, the assured confidence in the future which had made the first year of her married life almost a festival. Christmas was drawing near, and Jack and Tom were again to be their guests, but she knew that the girlish gaiety that had been so exuberant at Midsummer was as extinct as its flowers and fruits.

The one point that filled her mind, almost to the exclusion of every other, was the approaching vestry, and the action that Helstone had threatened to take. She had never given Karslake the warning with which she had been charged; it seemed to her a thing almost impossible to do, and she still clung to the hope that Helstone would abandon the intention.

But if that hope were fallacious! Julian must not be suffered to meet his enemy in ignorance of what awaited him. He must be told, and told by her, the shame and ruin that were preparing for him. Under this coercion he must give the explanation hitherto withheld, or what was the alternative?

She knew the character of the mixed crowd that made up the usual vestries at S. Mark's, and shuddered as her imagination suggested the details of the possible scene—the venom of the accuser, the stupefaction of the audience, to be succeeded by vulgar curiosity and noisy interpellation; and, worst of all, the inward suffering of the accused! He would bear himself—of that she was confident—with unshaken courage and constancy, but at what a cost?

Whether he justified himself, or refused to justify himself, the dignity and moral prestige of his position would be lost. There is, alas!

very little difference in the result, between suspicion and accusation and the desert of the
same ; the purity in either case is tarnished, and
the outside world stops to make no rigorous
analysis. At all risks, this public exposure must
be prevented ; and perhaps the best and most
legitimate method would be to induce her husband to confide his secret to her, and authorise
her to communicate it to Helstone, and thus
deprive him of his power of injury.   She would
do this at the first opportunity.

By this time, however, the boys had arrived,
and took up a good deal of her time and attention, besides reducing her hours of privacy with
Karslake to a very few. She was inclined to
think, also, that he availed himself of their presence to withdraw himself more and more into
the solitude of his library ; and on three several
occasions he had repeated his visit to the
mother and child, always informing her of the

fact, and expressing his unfeigned satisfaction at the boy's recovery, but with the most scrupulous abstinence from any word beyond the barest statement.

It was now within a week of New Year's Day, and he had excused himself from joining her and her brothers in some morning expedition, on the plea that he had a good deal of work to do at that time of the year, in the way of balancing accounts and regulating the distribution of the charities of the parish.

'But that is precisely the work, Julian, for which I have a special aptitude,' she answered, with a smile. 'After dinner I shall come in and help you.'

'You forget you have promised to take the boys to Covent Garden. You would not disappoint them of their pantomime?'

'I would disappoint them without hesitation to be of service to you—to bring back some of those happy working hours we used to enjoy together.'

'Used!' he repeated; 'is our happiness of the past, Sybil?'

She hesitated, knowing that at any moment Jack and Tom might rush into the room; this was not a suitable opportunity for the hard task she had before her. Still she might pave the way.

'It would be idle to say it has not suffered,' she answered gravely. 'Our love and trust may be the same as ever, but we have lost our light-heartedness. The question is, cannot we win it back?

He did not answer: if he had expressed what he felt it would have been a despairing negative.

'I have a matter to discuss with you when we have time,' she continued. 'Let us find time for it to-night, after we come home from the theatre and the boys are in bed. I wish you

would go with us, and we would make up the
arrears of work together. Could you sit out
the " Forty Thieves ? " '

'Yes,' he said, going up to her and kissing
with concentrated feeling the beautiful, beseech-
ing face, 'why not? I have taken no vows
against the innocent pleasures of the world. It
will do me a world of good to hear Jack and
Tom laugh, and you too, dear, I hope.'

There are few prettier sights than one of
our popular theatres during the Christmas
holidays. We do not refer to the splendour of
the spectacle or the almost noontide radiance
of the lights, but to the crowd of happy childish faces that look down from the front seats of
the boxes, or upwards from the stalls or pit :
some the dainty pets or curled darlings of fortune, all the source more or less of love, or
pride, or interest to the friends that have

brought them there. An atmosphere of good-
will and indulgence towards the children, of
sympathy with their delight—a softening reminiscence of the blessed days when we too were
young—seems to pervade the house, and the
sweet treble laughter rippling on all sides adds
a further element of purity.

Karslake's forethought had secured one of
the best boxes for his party, and Jack and Tom
were enjoying their privileges to the uttermost.
They were not town lads, blasé with juvenile
dissipations, contemptuous or even critical of
pantomimes. It was positively the first they
had ever seen, and the intensity of their interest
and zest of their enjoyment was proportionate.

Sybil had forgotten all her domestic
anxieties in her generous identification with
the rapture of her brothers, and was still more
oblivious of the attention excited by her own
exquisite face as she sat between them, un-

weariedly responsive to their enthusiasm. Her quiet toilette of ivory-toned silk, high to the throat, where it was edged by lace and pearls, harmonised perfectly with the character of her beauty.

Karslake, who sat behind them, soon became aware that their own box was becoming a centre of attraction, and he had risen to suggest that Sybil should change her place for one which enjoyed the doubtful privilege of the curtain, when it occurred to him it would be an infinite pity to disturb their enjoyment and introduce the disagreeable element of self-consciousness into her mind.

At that moment she was looking so radiantly happy that he almost caught the infection of her mood ; at least, he would not risk the spilling of one drop of her pleasure. So he sat down again, and watched the changes of her vivid face, and listened to her low murmuring laughter, with a passionate tenderness that seemed to gather concentration with reflection.

Was he, with his bondage to a miserable slavery, to be the blight of that full and joyous existence, when it had been the hope and purpose of his life, ever since he first saw her, to constitute himself the source and crown of her happiness? Her growing anxiety, her deepening gravity of late, caused him a pang of keenest compunction. What was possible to him towards the lifting of this burden he so unwillingly imposed? He dreaded the discussion she had proposed for that evening, for he knew that if it was her intention to touch the theme of his secret trouble, however tenderly or forbearingly, he must be subjected again to the exquisite torture of refusing her the satisfaction she wanted.

At this moment the curtain fell between the acts, and the boys turned eagerly round to talk to him. Sybil's attention, however, had become suddenly fixed; she was constitutionally so keen of vision as to be independent of an opera-glass, but now she slowly took up Julian's, which was lying close to her hand, and levelled it at the pit below. She gazed intently for the space of several consecutive minutes, and when she laid it down at length, it was not that she had gazed her fill but that she mistrusted the strength of her shaking hand.

'What is the matter, Syb—are you faint? What has made you turn so white all of a sudden?' cried Jack suddenly. 'Look at her, Julian!'

'A country girl never faints,' she answered, with a desperate effort to rally her firmness, but the more observant Tom interrupted her eagerly.

'It was something she saw down there!' pointing to the pit, and he pressed forward to

the front of the box and peered eagerly into the
abyss below. Julian came forward and looked
over his head.

He had stooped anxiously towards his wife
and questioned her with the tenderest anxiety,
but for once there was no response on her
part. She had withdrawn her pale face well
back now behind the shelter of the curtain, and
she neither raised her downcast eyes nor replied
by word or gesture. But as the power of the
shock subsided, and the fugitive blood returned
to her heart and cheek, she recovered sufficient
firmness to smile away the boys' vague concern
with some plausible explanation, and then she
concentrated her attention upon her husband,
as he swept the pit with his glass in search of
the key to her agitation.

But Covent Garden is a large theatre, and
not only was the pit densely crowded, but there
was the usual commotion of the going out and

coming back between the acts, and he seemed baffled.

Then came swiftly the flourish of instruments, the fanfare of trumpets; the curtain rushed up and the last act and crisis of the piece had begun. Jack and Tom, leaning over the box, forgot everything else in the culmination of the brilliant spectacle, and Julian stood motionless behind them, passing in patient review every face and figure below, within his range of vision.

Sybil, screened from observation, continued to watch him, and at length her heart leaped within her as she perceived his glass become stationary. He has hit the right focus—he is looking now at the lovely woman and lovelier child with whom their own fate seems so inextricably entangled.

What she had seen was this; a young mother take up her drowsy child from his place, and stand him upon her knees, evidently with the intention of rousing him up. The beauty of the girl and the tenderness which had accompanied the action, had first caught Sybil's attention, but as the boy, obeying the stimulus applied, shook back his golden curls and straightening his tiny figure, daintily clad in a picturesque costume, looked up and around him—the light from above seeming to fall direct upon his face—she felt as if she had received an electric shock. She could not analyse it; she could not say whether it were jealousy, doubt, or conviction: all she was conscious of was sharpest pain.

Karslake continued to hold the glass with unshaken firmness; he was well within the shelter of the box, and the objects of his attention were now intent upon the stage, or, if otherwise, had but feeble interest in the circles above them. He did not in any way blench or change colour, although he was quite aware his wife's pathetic eyes were on his face ; the lines of brow and mouth deepened a little—that was the only external sign. The inward sensation was that of a man who sees the resistless waters coming nearer, to overwhelm the point of safety on which he stands.

He put down the glass at length, and leant towards Sybil.

'Will you like to go home?' he asked.

She shook her head, glancing at the eager faces of her brothers, and then silence reigned between them. He sat down with folded arms and immovable face in the seat he had occupied before, and she tried to employ the interval in searching and regulating the chaos of her mind.

Presently he rose and went forward again to the front, taking the seat she had vacated, not, as her eager observation decided, for any other purpose than to engage the attention of

the boys and to cover her abstraction. In the
same way he succeeded, during the drive home,
in keeping them so actively employed with
the animated discussion of the pantomime that
Sybil's unusual silence passed unchallenged.
Jack, to be sure, sat holding his sister's hand in
his, and silently wondered what made her so
quiet, but it could be nothing very wrong when
she had been so merry an hour before, and
Julian had tucked all her shawls and wraps so
affectionately about her. She was so happy
with Julian, and he was such a good fellow.

'I will give the boys their supper, if you
would prefer to go to your room for a little
while,' he said, as he handed her out of the carriage. 'Do not think,' he added, with a slight
flush of colour as he met her grave examining
glance, 'that I wish to avoid the discussion you
spoke of: you can join me in the library
when they are gone to bed.'

'Thank you,' she answered, in a tone without emotion or inflection.

She went upstairs to her dressing-room, cheerful with shaded lamp and glancing firelight. Sybil had no professed maid,—it was a thraldom to which she could not submit,—so that no intrusive eyes were in attendance. She locked the door, threw off her cloak, and threw herself into the luxurious easy-chair drawn temptingly close to the fire, with a reckless abandonment of feeling such as she never remembered to have known before. Her state of mind was indefinable ; it seemed like dissolution or chaos.

Where was her inflexible belief? Some familiar words torn from their context seemed to haunt her mind with a weird appropriateness.

'I have heard of thee with the hearing of the ear, but now mine eye seeth thee.' What force did Helstone's denunciations and convic-

tions gather now that they were backed by the
deadly argument, recognised by herself, conveyed in the marvellous resemblance of that
child's beautiful upturned face!

O God! could he have deceived her? She
sat with her hands over her eyes to shut out
the light, and looked down mentally into the
abyss of that possible baseness—a baseness
than which there could be no lower depth. It
was to her agonised soul the very Valley of the
Shadow of Death, but after a space she struggled
through it to the light of day.

She could hear as she sat the light laughter
of the boys, and the occasional tones of
Karslake's voice, sweeter and clearer, and with
a truer ring than any other she had ever
known.

Oh, how the human voice speaks to
the living human heart! Slowly her hands
dropped restfully into her lap, and she felt her

stricken faith rise and quicken into renewed
fe.

After all, what did she know now that she
had not known before? Her husband's proud
denial availed as much over the evidence of her
material vision as over that of Gilbert Helstone's. Only it brought home with intense
power to her mind the cruel force of that fatal
and bewildering likeness, and supplied the most
stringent motives—nay, they were irresistible
—for pressing upon him the necessity of
explanation.

CHAPTER XXV.

AT this moment she heard the boys rushing
upstairs to bed, and knew they would not pass
without besieging her door.   She had just time
to turn the lock and open it before they reached
it, and to stand in the doorway to bid them
enter, her tall, white-draped figure irradiated
by the light within.

'O Tom! isn't this jolly?' cried Jack,
flinging himself on the hearthrug and basking
in the fire-rays like a spaniel; 'and Syb looks
like a fairy queen.'

' Of somewhat exaggerated dimensions,' returned she smiling, for she was gallantly bent

on sending them to bed without even the slightest cloud upon their brightness.

'Well, at least you'll own your life is like fairyland,' said Jack. 'I never knew what pretty things there were in the world before. This room, too! Think of your bedroom at Ashlands, Syb, with two wooden chairs and a big bath that we used to fill with water for you! And then, what a different thing it must be to live with Julian Karslake than father— I'm glad I know him!'

'He saved your life,' remarked Tom, who always considered this an incident of distinction; 'you ought to be fond of him.'

'I should like him just as well if he hadn't: —at least he didn't save Syb's life!'

He got up from the rug as he spoke and knelt at his sister's feet, with his elbows in her lap, his chin on his hands, and his bright eyes fixed on her face.

'There's one thing, dear, I can't quite make out—whether you always were so **very**, very pretty and we didn't know it, or whether you have grown so of late. Perhaps the lovely gowns make a difference.'

'Yes, Jack, that's the solution that I like best; but come, you must be off to bed!'

'I used to think,' continued Jack without moving an inch, 'that when I was a man, and had got on in the world, how I would pay you back for some of the hard work you did for us all. Now that is all over—you have everything that heart can desire!'

'Who knows?' said Sybil, shrinking involuntarily under the boy's eager words, as if they cast a foreboding before them. 'The future is always a sealed book, and no woman on earth can be so happy but a brother's love can make her happier. Come, Jack, you are getting pathetic, and I must insist on your taking your-

selves off. Did Julian give you a good
supper?'

'Oysters, mince pies, Stilton cheese, and
Burton—what would the youngsters at home
say?'

'Syb looks pale again, Jack,' remarked Tom.
'You're such a fellow to talk! Let's kiss her
and go to bed.'

At length they were gone, and now, late
as it was and weary as she felt, she had her
terrible task to perform. She knew that
under any circumstances sleep would have
been impossible without disburdening her
mind of its load. Only might she have grace
to do it without adding to his!

She went down-stairs very slowly. The
habitual elasticity of her step seemed gone, and
equally strange and unnatural was the set and
strained expression of her face. She opened
the library door without knocking; it was not

an intentional negligence, but an oversight of intense pre-occupation. Karslake was waiting for her there; he was standing by the fire leaning over the high mantel in an attitude habitual to him, facing the door as if watching for her entrance. He looked at her intently as she came in, placed a chair for her, and said :

'I have never seen you look so pale—you are as white as your gown. Sybil, what does it mean ? '

'That I am sick with anxiety, lest you should refuse the request I am going to make.'

'Yes,' he answered, in a tone of tender encouragement ; ' you know beforehand that any request of yours is granted as soon as preferred—if possible.'

She covered her eyes with her hands. An almost unconscious prayer went up from her heart to the Power outside and beyond herself; then she rose up and stood by his side.

'Julian, you know whom I have seen to-night, and what effect it has had upon me. I could not help it. My faith in you at this moment is firm as ever, or I should not be standing here ; but I do not deny that for a time it gave way under the sickening recognition of that lovely child's resemblance to yourself. You must not blame me for it—it was an instinct of physical perception that reflection and judgment corrected. Personally, I accept your assurances on this point implicitly, but I understand to-night as I never did before that it is almost a moral impossibility that others should believe you too. You are not angry?'

'No, I am not angry.'

'You will understand I allude to Gilbert Helstone, and you are very good,' with a faint smile, 'to bear the allusion so patiently. But you may be quite sure I should not name him without some very strong motive indeed.'

Karslake's feelings were something like those of a victim stretched on the rack, and awaiting the first turn of the screw.

'I quite understand,' he said gently. 'It is unnecessary to offer any assurance of the motives which influence you in this matter, dear. Tell me simply what you want me to do.'

'I want you to disarm Mr. Helstone's animosity. I want you to deprive him of the power of doing you a deadly injury.'

'As how?' he asked. 'My wife believes in me, what other injury can he do me? I can endure his misjudgment, and you must learn, Sybil, to do so too.'

She turned aside from the touch of his caressing hand: it was more than she could bear. Her next question seemed to him a strangely irrelevant one.

'Is the day fixed for the New Year vestry?' she asked.

'Not quite,' he answered, giving no expression to the surprise he felt. 'I find a note here from my churchwarden to-night, proposing January 4th as suiting the general convenience ; therefore it will suit mine.'

'In that case I must give you Mr. Helstone's message—one that he left with me that morning you found him here, and which I have kept up to this time because I have not had the courage or rather the cruelty to speak. But now there is no alternative.' She stopped, her voice choked with emotion.

'Spare me your tears, Sybil, if you can ; your distress tortures me.'

So did her hesitation, but he would not say that. He turned towards her, and passing his arm round her waist, he drew her close to his side.

'Tell me now,' he said, 'point-blank ! with as little attempt at softening as if Mr.

Helstone were here himself to dictate the words.'

'He says he will appear at the board in his right as parishioner, and lay before it a plain statement of the charges he has against you. He says, moreover, he can produce witnesses to support his testimony.'

She had obeyed and spoken; how would he receive it? For a moment she dared not raise her eyes to look at him, but involuntarily tightened her hold upon the hand which was passed round her waist.

He returned the pressure passionately but firmly, and this gave her courage to go on.

'Julian,' she urged, in a tone of intense pathos, 'this is to both of us a matter almost more than of life or death. You will put it out of Mr. Helstone's power to do this! I know how strongly you feel on the point, but you will not carry that feeling to the length of sacrificing all that we both hold dearest and most sacred! One duty is supreme till another overrules it, and your duty surely now is to defend your own honour—and more, the honour of the creed you profess. Forgive me, dear, if I seem to teach the teacher, or if I remind you that it is not only your happiness and reputation that are at stake. If I was slow to love at first I love you now with all the energy of my soul—my life is bound up in your welfare.'

She broke off and flung her arms round his neck.

' My God!' he exclaimed, shuddering back from the kisses she was laying on his pale lips, ' this is more than I can bear! Show me your way of escape, Sybil; I will take it if I can.'

' Tell me the story of this mother and child,' she answered with desperate abruptness, ' and give me leave to clear your character in Mr. Helstone's eyes.'

She withdrew herself from him as she spoke, and sank down again in the chair she had quitted, still keeping her eyes upon his face. Its expression of restrained feeling baffled her. She added, after a moment's pause, seeing that he remained silent :

'There is no other alternative, Julian. This man is simply bent upon your ruin because he believes in your guilt. Convince him of your innocence, and he will be eager to make atonement. And if it is some secret in which the honour of another is concerned, I know no more loyal nature than his. He could not betray a trust.'

'And yet my wife urges me to do so? If it were in my power to lay the whole truth before Gilbert Helstone, he would reject it. It would appear to him only another form of the fraud and lying with which he credits me. It must be enough for me, Sybil, that you do not ask for this guarantee as a condition of your own belief.'

She interrupted him. 'I do not ask you, Julian, to clear up this mystery personally to Mr. Helstone. Tell me the truth, and trust to my love and skill to convince him of your good faith. If you refuse——' she rose again as she spoke, moved by the irresistible impulse to approach him and overwhelm his evident reluctance by her caresses, but he drew back with a gesture of restraint and pain.

'I am constrained to refuse,' he said steadily, 'and do refuse. You love me, Sybil—your life is bound up in my welfare? Then you will cease to urge me on this point.'

'I do not know, I will not promise; your determination drives me to despair. Am I to understand you will suffer Mr. Helstone to fulfil his threat? You will face your vestry, three

days hence, with such an ordeal to meet? It is
not possible !'

'I have scarcely had time to consider all
the consequences that may ensue on my refusal,'
he answered, ' but they resolve themselves into
a question of endurance more or less. The one
thing I know to be impossible is to speak the
words that would clear this mystery. Whatever
the alternative I accept it—even to the wound-
ing of the happiness that is infinitely dearer to
me than my own.'

Every word, low as he spoke, fell clear and
unhesitating on her ears ; it was only the pallor
of his set face, and the strenuous grasp with
which his fingers closed over the back of a
chair near which he was standing, that indicated
the intense feeling he held in reserve.

' But,' she urged again, ' it is not a mere
question of your capacity for passively suffering
wrong. What do you think would be the

practical result of Mr. Helstone's accusation?
Would you propose to meet it with nothing
more than the miserable equivalent of a blank
denial? Julian, beloved! it would be of no use.
He would bear down your sweet rectitude with
his denunciations and proofs, and two-thirds of
your people would believe him, simply because
they could not understand any inducement
being strong enough to prevent you from esta-
blishing your innocence. Will you be able to
bear the consequences?'

He looked at her tenderly, with eyes, in
spite of his resolution, wet with tears.

'Will *you*?'

'No, she answered eagerly, 'I shall not!
If I see you robbed of the respect you have
earned and cast aside as guilty of this un-
paralleled baseness, I cannot bear it! And I
will go farther, even at the risk of displeasing
you. I will never give my consent to your

carrying out this act of reckless self-sacrifice to
such a bitter end.   Consider once more ; you do
not now stand alone in the world, and are
not justified in consulting only your personal
bias.   I claim to have my rights considered—
my right to the happiness and honour you
promised me ; my right not to be made a
forced participant in such a public shame and
scandal ! '

'That is an argument so powerful,' he said,
' that to resist it must convince you, if nothing
else will, of the uselessness of this controversy ;
and it is also so cruel a reproach that I scarcely
expected to hear it from your lips, Sybil.
Does your estimate of what I am rest on what
the outside world supposes me to be ? And when
its favour is withdrawn or exchanged for condemnation, will you refuse me the support of your
recognition and sympathy?   I own these are
contingencies I have not considered, but hard

as they are they even do not shake my resolution.'

'I am cruel,' she answered, raising her weeping eyes to the rigid calmness of his face, 'as a last resource to move you. If I forced my selfish interests upon you it was simply because I thought you might yield to these when proof against all else besides. In point of fact, your determination and all the trouble that may arise from it will, woman-like, only serve to quicken my devotion. Still I feel as if I could not give up my judgment in this matter and accept yours. Oh, that I knew what plea to use to win you to justice and to reason!'

'If,' he answered, for the first time turning from her, as if to hide the workings of his face, 'you will forbear to urge me any more I will take it as a proof of the love you still profess. Nothing that I may have to go through in the future can be worse than what I have borne

to-night.   In mere human pity do not say another word.   If you have thought me hard
and unresponsive to all the sweetness of your
appeals, it is because I should be lost if I were
to let you see what I suffer.'

As he spoke he sat down by the table near
him and covered his face with his hands.   She
went up to him and laid her hand gently on his
shoulder.

'You will still think me cruel to relentless-
ness,' she said, in tones of the most exquisite
tenderness, 'but one possible alternative occurs
to me.   There is time, between this and the
day fixed for the meeting, to see Gilbert
Helstone and try the effect of an appeal to his
forbearance.'

He lifted up his colourless face and looked
at her with stern surprise.

'Who is to make the appeal—you or I?'

'You,' she replied bravely, 'because my in-

tercession only serves to stimulate his bitterness. Julian, this is not a question in which
your conscience is involved. You will at least
sacrifice your pride for my sake—for the sake
of a possible reprieve! You will not refuse to
yield this little point?'

'Little! it would be a humiliation worse
than death, and it would be utterly in vain. Do
not ask it, Sybil!'

She remained silent, but she still stood by
his side as if awaiting his reaching a different
conclusion.

At that moment the clock on the mantel-
piece struck twelve : it was New Year's Day.

Karslake rose up with a deep sigh.

'I must send you away to rest,' he said, 'or
how will you meet the boys with a cheerful face
in the morning? It would be a mockery to
wish you " A Happy New Year." Would to
God I stood alone in this distress!'

'Do you remember last New Year's Day at Rome?' she asked, 'when we congratulated each other on being the happiest couple in the world?'

'I remember it, and accept all the reproach you imply. But I had never married could I have forecast the future. Try and believe this, Sybil; let me at least preserve your esteem!'

'And could I have forecast the future, Julian, I would still have married you in view of all this bitter pain. You are inexpressibly dearer to me now, in spite of being so stubbornly bent on your own undoing, than in the careless Roman days. If I ask you again on this New Year's morning to grant me a measure of relief by the sacrifice of personal feeling, will you refuse?'

He paused a few moments before he answered: even the tender, high-spirited girl that watched him had no adequate idea of the sharpness of the conflict.

'Well,' he said at length, in low reluctant tones, 'there is no escape from an appeal such as that. I dare not forego my duty at your intercession, Sybil, but I am at least free to accept my humiliation. I refuse no longer—I will go and see Mr. Helstone to-morrow.

CHAPTER XXVI.

It was not a seasonable winter; although the temperature was low the ceaseless rain fell from day to day. The holiday-makers were balked of their favourite pastime. There were no hilarious, excited thousands skimming over the Serpentine, with the ice like glass beneath their feet, and a cold blue radiant heaven overhead. The town was ankle deep in slush, and when the rain subsided the fog fell.

Julian Karslake had redeemed his promise to his wife, by calling at Gilbert Helstone's chambers in the Temple on the day following New Year's Day, but he was not to be found there. Julian left a message to the effect that he would call again at the same time on the morrow, but on this second occasion he was disappointed in not finding him at home.

The clerk who admitted him into the dingy room, and poked up the decaying fire, said that Mr. Helstone was not come yet, but had left word yesterday that he should be there in the course of the morning. Would the gentleman wait?

Yes, he would wait. And Karslake sat down, buttoning his overcoat tighter to keep out the penetrating cold, pulling his hat lower over his aching brows, and preparing to turn the delay to what account he could by renewed consideration of the matter before him.

One hour passed and another had almost run out before Helstone appeared, and then it was evident enough to Karslake that the delay had been employed as an intentional insult and annoyance rather than from any professional necessity.

'I do not profess to apologise for having kept you so long waiting,' he said, ' or to express any regret that you called here in vain yesterday—such conventional courtesies would be a mockery between you and me. I wish it had occurred to you to keep up the fire ; you are better guaranteed against the cold than I ; ' and he surveyed his visitor, with a sort of inclusive sneer, from head to foot.

A great deal is said about the ungenerous rivalries and ignoble jealousies of women, but the sterner sex have their kindred weaknesses, and to Gilbert Helstone the fine face and figure, and perfect bearing of his enemy, were always a fresh offence and provocation.

Karslake took off his hat, not so much from an instinct of civility, as the other retained his, but in some hope of relieving the oppression of his brain. If he had not been bound by his promise to Sybil, he would have left the office at once, so obvious was Helstone's intention to make his humiliation as bitter as possible. But though the failure of his attempt was a foregone conclusion, he had none the less to go through with it.

He stood up, and leaning a little over the high dust-covered mantel-shelf looked at Helstone, who had flung himself into a chair by his writing-table, and was leisurely balancing a paper-knife on his thumb, with the quiet steadfast glance habitual to him.

'I am told,' he began, ' it is your intention to be present at the vestry meeting to-morrow. Is it true?'

A cruel smile slightly curled Helstone's lips. He glanced keenly at the face of the speaker, and his heart quickened as he read in it the anticipated reward of his unwearied exertions.

'It is quite true : have you any objection to make?'

'I have no power to object, but, as a point of courtesy, I should be obliged if you would tell me the object you have in view.'

'I believe the meeting is merely a formal one, to pass accounts in connection with the distribution of charities at this festive season of the year, and that one of the churchwardens is to wind up the proceedings with a vote of thanks to the rector, for the special zeal and devotion he has displayed in the exercise of his functions. I have applied for permission to second the resolution.'

'Yes?' replied Karslake, somewhat mechanically.

'Oh! if you want to know in what terms I shall bear my testimony to your merits, you ask too much. I am not disposed to rehearse my speech in advance : your patience can bear the strain until to-morrow.'

'You seem to forget you have already instructed Mrs. Karslake to tell me the plan you have laid for my public humiliation and overthrow. I fully recognise your power to do me a deadly injury, and am here to-day, as I was yesterday, simply to ask you to forego your purpose.'

He spoke with so much quiet dignity, with such perfect abstinence from any word or tone that could give offence, that even Helstone felt its influence. He glanced sharply at him and hesitated before making his reply. Then he said :

'Well, there is one condition on which I will abstain not only from putting in an appearance to-morrow, but from any further interference in your affairs.'

He stopped again, and for a longer interval, with no other motive than to protract the painful suspense he knew he must be inflicting, but he did not succeed in extorting any indication of impatience. Karslake waited in undemonstrative silence till Helstone chose to proceed.

'If your wife will consent to leave you on the ground of the evidence of your infidelity which I have laid before her, I will abstain from placing the same proofs before any other tribunal. Otherwise I re-state them to-morrow.'

'And that condition I reject peremptorily, both on my own behalf and hers, let the consequences be what they may. If that is the only alternative you have to offer, the object with which I came to-day is already lost, but for all that I will state it. On the first occasion when you accused me in this matter I refused to give you any assurance at all as to my innocence, and since then my denial has been guarded and

reluctant. But now I am so coerced by circumstances, that I am prepared to assert in any way
you may demand that your conclusions are absolutely erroneous, and even to beseech you not
to drive me to this extremity.'

For a few moments Helstone remained silent,
with his gaze fastened on his companion, but his
cheek was flushed and his deep-set eyes shone
with excitement.

' This is a moment worth living for,' he said
at length, in a low concentrated tone, ' to see
your villany finding you out, and your pride
bowed to the point of abject entreaty. Does
an innocent man plead with a face blanched
with fear, and drops of perspiration on his brow?
I repudiate your denial as an audacious lie, and
reject your prayer with more contempt than I
can put into words. But I would have you take
notice that I have well redeemed the pledge I
made, as the redresser of Sybil Dorrimore's

wrongs, when we both stood by your pansy-
beds at Roosden Magna!'

'As a matter of fact, and in justice to my
own integrity,' replied Karslake, with invincible
composure, 'I repeat I have never wronged her
any more than that the request I preferred just
now was abject, or that guilt or fear had anything to do with the signs of disturbance unfortunately beyond my control.   To reduce me to
that point of humiliation, either now or to-
morrow, is beyond your power, Mr. Helstone.
I was led by the strongest considerations to
make a last appeal to your manliness of feeling,
and to warn you from doing an irremediable
wrong.   It has failed, but I am conscious of no
loss of self-respect because you are impervious
to the commonest instincts of humanity.'

'Good God!' exclaimed Helstone, springing
from his seat and approaching the dauntless
speaker with an almost menacing gesture, 'will

you brazen it out to the end, and add insult to unparalléled injury? But that end is close at hand. Don't delude yourself with any forlorn hope I shall relent at the last moment, for it is for this issue that I have schemed and laboured, or that I shall fail to carry my point and unmask your imposture! I have laid my plans with professional care—my brief is ready and conclusive. I am trusting nothing to the heat and uncertainty of vivâ voce controversy. After to-morrow, I defy Mrs. Karslake to keep her place under your roof.'

'I have nothing more to say,' said Karslake, taking up his hat; 'you will do your worst doubtless, but you will fail in one point of your programme, and the rest will be endurable.'

He went home slowly, walking through rain and fog the whole distance between the Temple and Bayswater. He wanted time to order his mind anew before he met his wife and told her of the failure of her passionate hope. He dreaded that absolutely as much, if not more, than the sickening experiences that awaited him on the morrow. The one point on which his mind revolved was the possibility of screening her from the full knowledge of the suffering he must of necessity endure : of the calamity she had a sufficiently adequate idea.

So terrible was the prospect before him, the infamous accusation which he dare not refute, the public shame from which he could not escape, that he began to reconsider with feverish anxiety whether there were no loop-hole of escape consistent with his honour.

But the conclusion reached was still the same despairing verdict : he was bound in the most absolute bonds ; he was pledged against trusting even the fidelity of his wife, whose fidelity, he well knew, would have been impregnable. There was no possible alternative or reprieve.

When at length he reached his home, jaded in mind and body, he went at once to the library.

'Ask Mrs. Karslake to come to me here,' he said to the servant. He knew how great her anxiety must have been during his absence, and was inclined to reproach himself for having protracted it so unnecessarily; he was now bound to tell her the result without any further delay. He soon heard her light foot on the stairs, and opened the door for her entrance, shutting it again before he prepared to speak to her.

But he had no need to speak; one glance into his face told Sybil her last hope had failed. A spasm of anguish contracted her heart as she looked at him.

'Forgive me,' she said, clasping his hand in hers, and drawing him towards the comfortable easy-chair, placed close to the cheerful fire, for she saw how weary he looked ; 'forgive me for sending you on such an errand.'

She sat down on a low seat at his feet, still holding his hand in hers, and scarcely conscious with what a convulsive clasp her slight, flexible fingers closed over it. And then silence reigned between them for a little while, she gazing steadfastly into the fire and trying to keep back the tears that glazed her eyes, and searching heart and brain in vain for some suggestion of comfort ; and he looking down upon her troubled face, and losing all sense of the misery of his own position in remorseful sympathy with hers.

Then to break the painful silence she asked a few questions. 'Had the interview been so very long ? how had Helstone behaved ?' and he, reflecting that she had never been present at any interview between them, and was happily ignorant of the aggravations of the same, answered with due reserve. But he did not deceive her in the least.

'What now remains,' he said, 'is to meet the inevitable with the best courage we can, and in order to do this I must have the night for consideration. The necessary preparations for to-morrow have been pushed by circumstances to the last moment, and I do not much regret it. The time that remains will suffice, and concentration and strength are best gained in the vigils of the night.'

'Do you mean you will sit up alone?

'Yes, solitude is necessary to my purpose. There are conditions of feeling beyond the reach of even your tender sympathy and love.'

She looked up at him with an expression of passionate, yearning pain.

'I see,' she answered, trying to hide the depth of her feeling under a smile; 'you are bracing yourself to the temper of martyrdom ! You are going to fortify your soul by all those spiritual aids which to me are so obscure, and to you so strongly efficacious. They may sustain you, Julian, till the hour of trial is over, seeing it is now so near, but when the re-action comes, and you see the ruin you have wrought, what then ? '

'Then,' he answered, 'I shall thank God He gave me courage to do the duty next to hand, without wasting my strength on the vain consideration of what would follow. But I go too fast, boasting as if I had already won the fight which may prove too hard for me after all.'

This was too much for Sybil's acquiescence ; her whole mind was in absolute revolt against the course of conduct on which he was re-solved, and it was with difficulty she could restrain her former importunity. She forbore, not so much from the conviction that it would be useless, as from her anxiety to spare him any measure of pain or even excitement of feeling in her power.

His present tone and manner, the sort of pale radiance that exalted the beauty of his face, the sense of what he had already submitted to for her sake that morning, so moved her tender sensibility, that she must either leave him to fight her own battle alone, or break down in some paroxysm of emotion.

Just then the dressing-bell rang, and she was glad of the excuse to rise at once.

'You must give me a dispensation from dinner to-day,' he said. 'I cannot eat, and I would rather not encounter your brothers' keen glances.'

'Fasting is a bad preparation for a long vigil, especially after sleepless nights.'

'On the contrary, it is the first step in the process ; but I will not insist on carrying it too far. Send me some soup in here, and I will eat it.'

'And you will lie down on the sofa and rest for an hour before the discipline begins; physical exhaustion won't add to your strength to-morrow.'

'You are right,' he said; 'I think I will, on condition that you do not let me sleep too long;' and she left the room a little comforted.

CHAPTER XXVII.

An hour after Sybil returned to the library, and found that Karslake had followed her advice, and was lying fast asleep on the sofa. In her nature there was a large measure of that tender protective compassionateness which has so much of the divine element in it; to relieve pain and suffering was the passionate bias of her soul. She stood for a few moments at his side, tracing in his face the lines of anxiety and care, which seemed more obvious in the collapse of slumber, with an intensity of sympathy that slowly grew into a resolute purpose.

Was there yet no escape? The meeting was fixed for noon the next day, but there were

still some hours of possible effort before her.
What could she do?

Helstone had hardened his heart against
Julian's appeal, and she had small hope that
hers would be more effectual, but at least she
could try. His house was only a short distance
from theirs, and she had all the fearlessness of a
country girl in regard to walking alone. At
that hour, too, she would be most likely to find
him at home; also she would enlist Sara's
sympathies in her behalf—of what avail was
any further reserve in view of the morrow's
eventualities? Then it suddenly flashed upon
her mind that, in his last interview with her,
Helstone had alluded to some possible alternative he might be induced to offer her. In
that case her husband's honour was secure, for
there was nothing that could be claimed from
her of personal sacrifice that she would not be
prepared to surrender.

She decided not to let anyone know of her going out. She had induced her brothers to sit down to a little steady school-work for an hour or two, on the plea of returning to the library, and they would think her still shut up there; while, on the other hand, when Julian awoke, he would believe her to be with them. She went out of the room softly, with a parting glance of ineffable tenderness at the sleeper, but refraining from touch or kiss, lest she should wake him.

She let herself out into the road through one of the side entrances of the house, not venturing to risk attracting attention by opening the front door. It was still raining, and the few scattered lamps of the district burned with a dim lurid light through the murky air. The foggy atmosphere seemed to enclose her; there was no visible heaven above or earth beneath. Keen as her vision was, and acute as were her

perceptions of locality, it was with some difficulty she succeeded in finding the house she
wanted in Burnham Square.

The maid that admitted her beamed a surprised welcome, for she knew Sybil well.

'Are your master and mistress both at
home?' she asked, and without any attempt to
conceal the anxiety she felt as to the reply.

In a moment the little sitting-room where
Sara usually sat when alone was opened, and
she herself hurried out into the hall to greet
her guest.

'Sybil, my dear, is it you? So late, and on
such a night! but come in, come in; you are
more welcome than words can express.'

She insisted on taking off her wet cloak with
her own hands, and sending it to the kitchen to
be dried, with many implicit instructions to the
maid; and then she drew her inside the cosy little
apartment with which Sybil was so pleasantly

familiar, made her sit down by the fire, and was even hospitably bent on taking off her wet boots.

But this Mrs. Karslake would not allow.

' They are not wet through, I assure you, and I shall not have time to stay very long ; but how good of you to be so pleased to see me ! '

' Good ! ' repeated Sara, who had now subsided into a seat on the other side of the hearth, planting her own feet firmly on the fender, as an encouragement for her visitor to do the same. ' Why, child, you forget I never go out and speak to my kind as other people do. Besides, you are a special favourite of mine; but I thought you had been forbidden to come here.'

' I have never been forbidden; it is your brother's conduct which has made it impossible till now. I hope he is at home ? '

' Yes,' said Sara, dropping her voice a little, ' he is still sitting over the dinner-table; he drinks more wine than he used to do, and I'm afraid the tempers of neither of us improve.'

Sybil lifted up her beautiful face full of tender sympathy.

'Do your troubles increase?' she asked, with as profound a pity for the harassed woman before her as if her own heart were not sick with care; 'are things worse than they were? is he as good as ever?'

'I think he is as good as ever—to *her*,' she answered with a short laugh, ' but certainly not to me. He cannot bear contradiction, and will not forgive me for not abusing Mr. Karslake as he does. But, my dear, I am not quite going to believe that you came here to-night to ask after our troubles—they stand pretty much as they were. Tell me what makes you look so pale and sad—you have not quarrelled with your husband?'

Sybil shook her head with a conclusive smile, but it was such a pathetic one that Miss Helstone felt the tears rise to her eyes.

'Can you tell me what is the matter, my dear?'

'I am come on purpose to tell you everything, and to ask your advice; but '—with a sudden flush of painful crimson—'you know what your brother's charge against my husband is?'

'Not exactly, I have never cared to press the point; it is some breach of morality, of which I am certain he is as innocent as myself. We will take that for granted.'

'No, we will take nothing for granted,' said Sybil, in a low voice, 'it will be necessary for you to hear a long story.'

She looked at her watch; it was eight o'clock.

'Can I depend on seeing Mr. Helstone later?

He will not go out?' she asked the question
with intense anxiety.

'He cannot go out of the house or even
leave the room opposite without our hearing
him,' said Sara, 'and I would stop him at once.
That is right!' as Sybil moved near to her;
'come and sit on the cushion at my feet; contact gives confidence, and my whole heart will
go with you, my dear.'

Thus encouraged, and in defiance of strong
natural reluctance, Sybil told her story, and Sara
listened with her keen perceptions all on the
alert and, it must be confessed, with an ever-
increasing sense of dismay and astonishment.
There was no attempt made by the wife to
reduce or soften the evidence against her husband; she gave the facts as blankly as Helstone
himself could have done, feeling that perfect
sincerity was the only condition of success. At
length she reached the culminating point—

Helstone's determination to bring the matter before the next day's vestry, and her strenuous hope of being able to win him from his purpose.

So ominous a silence fell as Sybil ceased to speak, that she turned round with pained surprise to look into her friend's face.

Sara was sitting with brows knitted and lips compressed into an expression of stern perplexity. As the girl looked up she suddenly bent over her, raised her face between her hands, and gazed into it with piercing inquiry.

'And you believe in your husband's fidelity with that clear head of yours—not with the blind infatuation of too fond a wife? It is hard to understand!'

'What do you take me for?' asked Sybil, with a gesture of proud self-assertion. 'Am I a likely woman to condone offences such as these—offences that would involve a depth of baseness difficult to calculate? I believe in his honour as I believe in my own. I trust him as I trust in God.'

Sara looked at her with a cynical yet kindly smile.

'And you love him, child, with that extravagance of feeling that you may well pause, and ask whether your judgment is free enough for an unbiassed opinion.'

'My love is not extravagant,' replied Sybil, in a voice of indignant pain, 'but is rather the slow and reluctant fruit of conviction and reason. I have lived in as close intimacy with Julian Karslake as is possible for a wife to live with her husband, and know him to be without reproach. Without reproach! that is a poor way of expressing what I have learnt and proved of the sweetness and strength, the tenderness and patience of his character. If I did not love him now with all the faculty of loving

that I have, it would be because I was blind or
insensible. And do not imagine that I am
influenced by the beauty of his person, or the
charm of his manner—they would not move
me apart from this real goodness—though I
grant,' she added in a lower tone, ' they help
to make daily intercourse a privilege and a
delight.'

'My dear,' said Sara, ' all that is very fine
language, but just means, in my vernacular,
being over head and ears in love; and that
again means you must be on your guard
against being blinded by the strength of your
feelings. This is a very serious business.'

'And you incline to believe there is justification for your brother's conduct?'

'Whatever I believe,' said Sara gravely,
' can stand over for future consideration. The
night grows late, and I am almost as anxious
as you are that Mr. Karslake should be spared

this public exposure. Will you go in to Gilbert alone, or shall I ask him to come to you
here?'

'I would rather see him here, in your presence;' but her heart sank at the prospect
before her, for Sara's lack of faith seemed a
new proof of the strength of the evidence
against her husband. If a staunch supporter
of his cause could doubt so easily, what could
be expected of the indifferent outside world?

Sara was absent longer than might have
been expected, and Sybil could not help hearing their voices in angry discussion. Presently
she came back with a heavy, sullen look.

'He refuses to see you unless you go to
him, my dear; he will not come here or talk
before me. Will you do so?'

'Certainly; I will go,' said Sybil, rising at
once, 'there is no other choice.' Sara went
over to her side and kissed her.

'God bless you, my dear Sybil!' she said solemnly, and to the poor girl's excited mind there seemed a foreboding in the benediction.

Helstone was seated at the table with wine and nuts before him, and he had already drunk enough to disturb the perfect equilibrium of brain and temper. As Mrs. Karslake crossed the room so as to approach the place where he sat, and he marked the swift grace of her movements and the beauty of the pale sad face, which seemed to gain some new charm of expression every time he saw it, he felt the hot blood rush to his brow, and said to himself that this time he should not be able to hold his passion in check.

'You were not afraid to come and speak to me alone?' he said, placing a chair for her.

'I was not afraid,' she said, coldly; 'it is a feeling of which I have little experience. I should have liked Sara to have been present simply because I wanted her help. You know why I am come ? '

Her voice fell from the pitch of womanly dignity, with which she had begun, to the thrilling pathos of a despairing appeal. She lifted her eyes, wet with unshed tears, and pushed back the heavy weight of her abundant hair from her brows, with a gesture familiar to him from her childhood when she was in trouble.

' I do not know,' he replied hoarsely; ' you must tell me.'

' To renew the request you have already refused,' she said more firmly ; ' to ask you to drop this persecution of my husband.'

The word stung him to the quick ; the very pallor of her face, the vibrations of love and suffering in her voice, and the anguish of her glance, hardened his heart against her. If she had loved him less her chance would have been greater.

On the table, close to his hand, lay a thick packet sealed and addressed. He called her attention to it.

'This is my answer,' he said; 'I am going to forward this packet by to-night's post to Mr. Karslake's churchwarden, with the request that before the vestry meets he will try and communicate its contents to his brother official. It contains a dry professional statement of the evidence I have at command in proof of his immorality before marriage, and his infidelity afterwards. Those finer traits of infamy and fraud, through which he has succeeded in reducing your mind to a state of slavish credulity, I have not insisted on—the public need not be invited to discuss that matter. I have done this, Sybil, to make the object I have in view the surer—the exposure of the most shameless impostor one could meet with in a lifetime, and a woman's deliverance from a degrading bondage.'

She passed over all there was of offence in his speech; the facts alone moved her.

'But you will not send it! I do not argue nor even plead for Julian, only for myself! The happiness of my life hangs on this point. Spare him for my sake—for the sake of the old days at Ashlands, when you were my best and kindest friend.'

She went up to him and laid her hand on his arm; he shook it off almost fiercely.

'Sit down, Sybil, for mercy's sake! If this man were common cheat or libertine I could forgive him; but he has cajoled and betrayed a girl who was and still is to me the dearest and most sacred thing on the face of God's earth, and of whose honour I think more by countless lengths than my own. Every word you utter in his favour only confirms my resolution. I am going to save you in spite of yourself.'

She was silent; he went on again.

'I have told you before I have laid my plans carefully. The shock of indignation and surprise would have been too much for the meeting, without some steps of preparation. Now his churchwardens will come primed with facts and fury, and will be eager to listen to what further statements I shall have to make. Possibly, also, each man will have bruited the scandal to his nearest neighbours and friends, for I have given no hint at secrecy. Julian Karslake will find himself in a new atmosphere, charged with suspicion and outraged decency, instead of favour and respect. Don't deceive yourself, Sybil, with the idea that they will not believe it—that his immaculate character will speak for him. To prevent any reaction in his favour that his excellent acting might produce,

I shall clinch the matter by ocular demonstration.'

Sybil's cheek blanched with terror; it was with difficulty she could repress a cry of pain.

'What do you mean?' she gasped.

'I mean that I shall show the child to the meeting. It is a theatric touch that I personally dislike, but rather than Julian Karslake should escape the full weight of his shame I will stoop to it. I have made friends, or affected to do so, with the boy. His poor simple-hearted mother knew that on one occasion I followed your husband to her house, and imagines consequently that I am his friend; so there has not been much difficulty. I spare her——' his heavy brows contracted ominously. 'I will spare you too,' he added, glancing at the anguish-stricken wife, 'and could almost feel a disdainful pity for the man himself in the crisis of his downfall.'

For a few moments Sybil sat motionless, crushed with despair. It was all true; the completeness of the disgrace would exceed her worst apprehensions—it would be absolute. Julian brought face to face with that fatally gifted child would, indeed, be at the mercy of his relentless enemy.

Helstone sat watching the changes of her face with glowing eyes; presently he rose and approached the bell.

Almost with the swiftness of light she sprang from her seat, and intercepted his intention. 'What are you going to do?' she demanded.

'Simply to despatch my letter to the post. Do you still hope to circumvent my purpose?'

'O wait!' she cried passionately, 'it must not be done—he could not bear it! You spoke before of an alternative. Show me any way of deliverance, and I will accept it!'

He seemed to hesitate, and taking out his

watch, looked at the dial. 'I have not much time for parley,' he said harshly, 'nor shall I try as I have done before to win you to a sense of womanly dignity. Here is my alternative. If you will pledge your word to leave your husband, on the sufficient grounds of his wrongs against you, I drop my persecution : that is, I fling this letter in the fire, and suffer him to cheat his followers to the end of the chapter !'

'Leave him ! I do not understand.'

'As you please. I am indifferent as to your decision. The pressure of social opinion will constrain you to do ultimately what you now refuse; the only difference being that in the one case you keep your idol on his pedestal.'

He spoke quietly, but every pulse in his body throbbed with excitement. To rob Julian Karslake of the woman he himself

adored, and of whom the other was utterly
unworthy, would be a keener rapture of vengeance than even his public humiliation.
Hitherto the younger man, with his gifts of fortune and nature, had forestalled, circumvented,
and beaten him—had appropriated, enjoyed,
but not exhausted that experience of blessedness
he had so silently but strongly desired for
himself. Not exhausted—no! He had never
trusted himself to see them together since their
marriage, but he knew, if only from the young
wife's manifestations, how close was the bond
of union between them, and what would be
the intolerable hunger of the soul—the blank-
ness of desolation that must follow on its
rupture.

He still stood with the letter in his hand
and his eyes on his watch; furtively he watched
Sybil. He had said more than once that he
chose for her misery rather than shame, but

the misery was more intense than he expected, and though it did not shake his purpose one iota it cost him almost more than he could bear to restrain the expression of his own feelings.

Only, he knew that one hint of his selfish passion would rob him of his revenge.

'You will think me very hard,' he said, breaking the silence, 'but in five minutes' time I must close this miserable controversy; that is, I shall despatch my letter if you do not give me the pledge I require.'

'I do not quite understand,' answered the unhappy girl, passing her hand over her eyes as if to clear her troubled vision. 'For how long am I to leave him ? where am I to go ? '

'For how long ? ' he repeated. 'For just as long as his reputation is of the same account in your estimation as it is to-day; for as surely as you return to him, or even, however slightly, break the pledge of utter separation, so surely shall I take up the business of public exposure, precisely where I lay it down to-night. As for where you should go, you will have plenty of friends to advise you on that point.

She stood before him, erect, motionless, her hands clasped with almost convulsive stringency, her dilated eyes gazing straight before her, as if into the blackness of the darkness of the terrible future. Then an involuntary shudder shook her from head to foot; she brought her gaze slowly back on Helstone's face.

'Have pity!' she said, with a gesture of desperation; 'my life is bound up in his!'

'Enough!' he answered, clenching his teeth beneath his thick moustache with a spasm of vindictive hate; 'the die is cast. I will leave you to do my own business. It is too late now to trust the slackness of a servant.'

He took up the letter, and moved towards the door. As he expected, she again intercepted him.

'Destroy the letter,' she said, in a voice strained and unnatural, 'and repeat your promise that you will cease to molest him now and for ever!'

He did not respond at once; he had to regulate the rush of almost overwhelming feeling. Then he answered, quietly:

'So let it be. I will trust your honour, Sybil Karslake.'

He approached the fire and threw the letter into it.

'What am I to do next?' she asked, almost wildly. 'Will you bind yourself by some oath? will you require one from me? I shall not give it! My pledge can go no farther than this, that I leave him now to save him from a dishonour worse than death, but that I cannot depend upon myself. I am not strong enough to bear self-inflicted pain as he does, and if my misery is too much for me I shall go back.'

'The bargain is conditional,' he said coldly. 'Go back if you will, and you know the result. The fact of your having left him at all will be so much additional evidence against him. But stay! where are you going now?' he asked, as she turned from him as if with the intention of leaving the room.

'Home!' she replied sternly. 'Did you imagine I should consent never to see him again?'

'That requires consideration,' he said, beginning to pace the room in excitement. 'Final embraces, passionate adieus, form no part of my programme. Moreover,' turning sharply round and stopping before her, 'he will not let you go—if you tell him. He will prefer to drag you down into the slough of his own dis-grace.'

'No,' she replied, with a brave effort to conquer herself and speak calmly, ' he would not let me go, therefore he must not know that I am going.'

She stood in deep reflection for a few moments; then lifted her stricken face with a proud composure which moved him to the depths of his being.

' I will tell him nothing; he does not know I am here. We will meet and part as usual until to-morrow. He will go to the meeting, braced to met you there, and will find that his good name is still spared to him. Before his return I will leave the house.'

She turned from him and went out into the hall. Sara came forward to meet her, and tried to draw her back into her own room, but in vain. She was frightened at the aspect of her face and the desperate calmness of her manner.

'Will you not tell me what has passed?' she asked.

'I cannot; ask him. Kiss me; you have been very kind to me.'

'You shall not go home alone, my dear. Wait just two minutes, and I will have on my cloak and bonnet. I could not sleep if I did not see you safe under your own roof.'

Sybil shuddered involuntarily. 'I can wait,' she said mechanically, and stood in the same spot, passive and motionless, with arrested sensation, till her friend joined her.

Not a word was spoken during the brief journey: the fog had lifted, a few stars gleamed in the sky, but had there been portents in heaven Mrs. Karslake would not have seen them.

She parted from Sara a few paces from her own door.

'Do not go any further!' she urged, and the other forbore to dispute the point, and left her but half-satisfied, for she had not seen her safe under her own roof after all.

Sybil walked round swiftly and silently to the side entrance, which she had left ajar on leaving the house. To her relief it yielded at once to her hand, and she effected her return as she had done her departure, without observation.

The servants were supping solemnly with closed doors; she heard the sound of her brothers' cheerful voices in the dining-room as she sped upstairs; probably they had not left it all the time.

All the time! How long was it?

She had now reached the shelter of her dressing-room, but before looking at her watch she took off and put away carefully the hat and cloak she had worn.

She had been absent an hour and a half. It seemed to her, as she stood there in her blank, unutterable misery, a cycle of torture.

At least, it had been long enough to wreck her life.

CHAPTER XXVIII.

The boys went to bed that night without seeing their sister. They thought she was working with Julian at the accounts in the library, and contented themselves with singing a cheery goodnight outside the door, to which, however, he only responded.

Sybil was lying face downwards on her bed, prostrate with misery, passively suffering the waters of her affliction to flow over her. She could not think, I was going to say she could not pray ; but surely the extreme sacrifice she was offering, the speechless appeal of her breaking heart to some power outside her own weakness, partook of the nature of prayer.

She had no interruption to provide against. Julian was going to spend the night down-stairs, but would he not expect to see her again and bid her good-night? If he did it was impossible. All her secret would escape her at the first tones of his voice, even if her face, marred with tears and uncontrollable emotion, did not disclose it in advance. All she could hope was that the hours would bring some degree of calmness and courage, and then, as it drew towards morning, she would bathe and change her dress and go down to him. But the hours of the night passed, and the anguish of the unhappy wife seemed to augment rather than to slacken.

Thought and memory were hard at work in the torture chamber of her brain. She found herself recalling every incident in connection with her husband, from the first casual meeting in the village street, when she remembered she had involuntarily turned to look a second time

at the most beautiful face she ever remembered
to have seen, to the last glance she had taken
of him that evening. The incidents of their
singular courtship; her own reluctance and coldness; his strength and sweetness, that had so
slowly won their way, and his unlimited goodness to her family, came back in vivid detail.
And since? What tenderness could have been
more perfect—what courage and constancy
greater than his in all the troubled relations of
the past?

Well, here at least she could emulate him.
He was willing to sacrifice his honour to his
honour—his integrity to his integrity—even
to take the ruin of his life rather than forego
what he held to be his bounden duty. And she,
was not she making an equal, nay, a costlier
sacrifice?

At twenty years of age she was offering up
the spring and blossom of her life in order that

shame might not touch him.   What more was possible to saint or martyr? What, indeed, were mere physical tortures to the long agony that stretched before her? And then—the crowning pity of it!—she was at the same time inflicting as much as she spared. And so the night wore on in paroxysms of speechless pain.

At length she heard the clock strike six. The darkness at that hour was, of course, still absolute, but it told her how few hours were left of those she was free to spend with him. She rose from her couch of anguish, bathed in ice-cold water as her custom was, changed her dress, and, by the light of the candle she held, examined her looks with melancholy solicitude She had never seen herself look so ill and changed. But what did it matter? he would scarcely expect a cheerful face.   Still she spent a few minutes in putting appliances to her aching eyes and head, and then sat for another quarter of an hour motionless in her chair, heedless of cold, to give them time to take effect. She would have sat longer, but her strained ears caught the sound of the quiet opening of the library door. He was probably coming up-stairs—she must go and meet him. She went out, and stood at the head of the stairs to receive him.

'You were going to your room to lie down till breakfast time?' she asked, in a voice that sounded to her own ears of an unnatural quietness, and with a feeling little short of despair at her heart, lest such should indeed be his intention, and she deprived of just so much of their brief companionship.

He held a lamp in his hand, which irradiated his face while her own remained in deep shadow; but she saw with an involuntary pang how much of his habitual aspect he had. recovered. ,

'O no!' he answered. 'I feel no need of sleep. I am simply going to my dressing-room. But why have you begun the day so early? and,'—coming close to her and touching her hand,—'my sweetest girl, how pale and ill you look! Have you been sitting up, too, wearing out your heart for me? Remember, Sybil, that is about the only reproach I cannot bear; that cuts at the very root of my courage. You are cold too; go down-stairs, there is still a good fire in the library—you make me ashamed of the comfort I have enjoyed—and I will join you in half an hour.'

He would have returned with her, but she objected.

'There is no need, it would be losing time—only make haste!' she said. She went down alone, he standing to light her way till she had entered the room below and closed the door. She stood still in the centre of the

floor, and looked about her with nervous
eagerness. She wanted to see if she could
discover how he had spent the night.

The soft astral lamp was still burning, and
the fire fairly good ; the writing table had much
the same appearance as when she saw it last
the evening before ; the accounts that wanted
attention were still untouched—he had evidently not done much work. There was a little
old-fashioned Latin copy of the ' Imitation ' of
Thomas à Kempis in the chair where he usually
sat. She took this up, straining it with both
hands against her lips, and then slipped it into her
pocket. She went up to the couch where he
had lain, and leaned her cheek on the pillow,
but she felt the convulsive sobs rising in her
throat. Such self-indulgence would be his
ruin !

Then it occurred to her that he must be
faint with mental exhaustion and hunger, having

scarcely tasted food the day before. The servants would not be up for another hour. She would prepare some coffee with her own hands. Since she was married she had never had the pleasure of serving him—that privilege was reserved for hirelings—but now here was her opportunity! The idea for the moment banished her despair.

The coffee itself was generally made in a French *cafetière*, so perfect in construction as to leave little to the skill of the cook ; but there was the canister to seek in the housekeeper's closet, and the kettle to fill. Her trembling fear was she would find the receptacle locked, as it doubtless ought to have been ; but the best of servants are not infallible, and she blessed the good woman for her happy negligence as she felt the door yield to her touch. In the same place she discovered some tea cakes and butter, perhaps intended for private con-

sumption, but she carried them off with her,
with almost a glow of pleasure, as well as
the dainty copper kettle, already considerately
filled, which Mrs. Norris never suffered to
leave her own apartment.

When Karslake came down, refreshed by
his bath and change of dress, and full of
quiet strength of mind and purpose, there was
an embroidered cloth on a tiny Chippendale
table, spread with all the usual appliances for
breakfast, and Sybil, kneeling on the rug before
the fire, was picking up the cinders from the
hearth with discriminating fingers, and dropping
them with anxious attention into the cavities
of the fire.

'There is no more coal,' she said, looking
back towards him as he entered, 'and the
kettle will not boil! Do not be shocked. I
have often done this at Ashlands; we did not
waste cinders there.'

It was an unfortunate allusion; her voice choked in sobs.

He went up to her and bent over her.

'You break my heart, Sybil,' he said. 'I reproach myself that you have suffered alone last night.'

For reply she turned and kissed him, with a lingering passionateness alien to her general manifestations, and very hard for him to bear with equanimity. Her mood perplexed and troubled him.

'May I help you?' he asked presently, as he saw her preparing to lift the now boiling kettle with her delicate hands; 'surely that is too heavy!'

'You little understand what duties I fulfilled in the old times at home,' she answered, with a desperate effort to rally her firmness. 'We should have considered this an elegant toy then and there, and it is my wish to wait upon you this morning to the minutest point. No! do not rise. I will bring it to you when it is ready. Is not the aroma reviving, and are not you faint for want of food ?'

She spoke rapidly and constantly, fearing to be silent lest her emotion should conquer her again, and trying to concentrate her attention upon inducing him to eat and drink in a measure proportioned to her impression of his necessities. He was soon satisfied, however, and she only sipped and could scarcely swallow her cup of coffee. Strong emotion, and especially restrained emotion, is not conducive to appetite.

Then he proposed they should go through the accounts together.

'There is some hours' work to be done,' he said, 'and I shall not be able to get through it alone. I thought of doing it last night, and half expected you would have come in and offered to help me; but you were quite right to stay with the boys. They need know nothing of to-day's business, Sybil!'

'No,' she answered, in a voice scarcely audible, 'they need know nothing.'

He looked at her again with distressed anxiety; but now she was drawing her chair to the writing-table, adjusting the drooping lamp, and beginning to look over his papers, but with so little of her usual sweet composure.

'Will the meeting have patience to attend to all these minutiæ,' she asked nervously, 'when the excitement will run so high on your personal affairs, Julian?'

'All these formalities will be settled first, or, whether they are or not, they must at least be in a condition to bear the strictest investigation.'

'I understand,' she answered, with her tender smile; 'trust me, I will make no mistakes.'

They worked together for a couple of

hours without interruption; her mind was now absorbed in her task. It was the last service she would probably perform for him, and if the strain upon taxed brain and opposed inclination had been greater, she would have been equal to its exercise. Long before they had finished the house grew full of light and movement; the servants were moving to and fro in their allotted functions; the boys rushed downstairs and begged for admittance, and then there was the inevitable adjournment for breakfast.

Sybil sat behind her urn and distributed the cups, but more than this she could not do, pleading a violent headache.

She left Karslake to cover her mental prostration by engaging her brothers' attention in the discussion of which of several plans was the best for their amusement in the day before them, but she perceived at the same time his unrelaxed solicitude for herself. The drawn look of suffering upon her face was greater than any ordinary physical pain could have produced. He little knew that the one cry of her soul, as she followed his every word, glance, or gesture, took the form of the hopeless wail, 'The last time! the last time!'

When the meal was over, and Jack and Tom had gone out on some boyish business of their own, he asked her to come back to the library, now duly swept and garnished, with fire cheerfully replenished, and all traces of irregular uses removed.

'You must do no more work, Sybil, beloved!' he said. 'I was to blame to suffer it before breakfast; but if you will lie down on the sofa while I write, I shall at least have the sweet comfort of your presence.'

She acquiesced. It was the best thing she could desire to lie and look at him till her weary eyes drooped with the tension of her gaze, while he worked on unconscious, or seemingly unconscious, of her fixed regard.

After a time he brought his task to a conclusion, rolled up his papers, and, rising from his seat, looked at his watch.

'It is eleven o'clock,' he said, coming up to her; 'in another hour I must be in S. Mark's vestry-hall. Sybil, is it the dread of what may happen there that distresses you so much?'

'In another hour?' she repeated.

'Are you afraid,' he continued, sitting down beside her, and taking one of the feverish little hands, that lay outside the soft crimson blanket that covered her; 'are you afraid that I shall lose my self-command under Mr. Helstone's provocations, or succumb to the adverse feeling he may excite against me? I trust in God I shall do neither! Besides I have the stimulus of your faith, and shall have the consolation of your sympathy.'

Sybil could scarcely repress a sob of agony. The sickness of her heart, the terrible demand upon her self-repression made her physically faint, only she would not have lost the consciousness of his sweet presence for a moment. She raised herself from her recumbent posture, and passing her arm round his neck, leaned her throbbing temples upon his breast. He drew her closer, with intense but restrained tenderness.

'I know well,' he said gently, 'that you think I am committing an error of judgment— sacrificing our united interests to some exaggerated notion of honour, perhaps to some disguised form of pride. Sybil, I have spent the hours of the night in as rigid an examination of conflicting motives and duties as I am capable of, and I am calmly confident I am doing right. Only it would be an additional help and comfort if I could win your approval as well.'

Her only answer was a passionate pressure of the hand she held. What could she say, poor suffering soul?

'Will you go to your room, and try and sleep away your pain as soon as I am gone?' he asked presently. 'Let me carry you up-stairs! I had thought of taking half an hour's walk before I go into the hall.'

'Oh, do not go!' she rather breathed than spoke. 'My head aches too much for change of place; let me stay here!'

He drew her closer in his arms and stroked her bowed head caressingly. She was so quiet he almost thought she slept, while every faculty and sensation were stretched on the rack of endurance. She was counting the tickings of the clock with almost delirious anxiety. At length the quarter to the hour chimed.

'I must leave you now,' he said, putting her gently from him ; 'it would not do to be late.'

He rose as he spoke and she rose too, moved she hardly knew by what impulse. He took both her hands in his, and kissed her quietly on the forehead ; his great desire being to soothe the intense excitement under which he saw she was labouring.

'My darling, I shall probably not be two hours absent.'

A spasm passed over her white, set face. Then, with a great effort, she commanded her voice enough to speak.

'Have I ever vexed you, Julian, or disappointed or grieved you in any way, since we were married? If I have, say you forgive me!'

He looked distressed. 'Never! You have been the sweetest and most loyal of wives as

well as the most beloved. Rather it is for me to
ask that question.'

She turned her eyes away from him with a
long shuddering sigh, but still keeping her hold
upon his hands.

'You are impatient to be gone,' she said,
'and I will not keep you any longer.   Kiss me
once more, Julian, and then go, while I have
strength to give you leave to go.'

CHAPTER XXIX.

LIFE is full of pathetic suggestions, and amongst the most significant is the apparent waste of human power and effort. The trial that over-whelms us is precisely that special misfortune which we never expected or provided against; the blow that crushes us is dealt from some quarter where our confidence was most implicit. We spend our strength in fortifying our souls against some supreme loss or evil, the antici-pation of which clouds half a lifetime perhaps, and the shadow passes over and touches us not. There are hundreds of men and women, who sap the healthy springs of existence by corroding anxieties respecting events which never become part of their actual experience.

For the most part, blessing or cursing, the rapture of fruition or the bitter pain of frustration, comes upon us unawares, or in some guise so different from what we expected that we have not the faculty to recognise it. In brief, 'it is always the unforeseen that happens.'

Some such reflections as these occupied the mind of Julian Karslake as he walked down the steps of S. Mark's vestry-hall, surrounded by cordial friends and pleasant greetings, at the close of the meeting for which he had braced his powers of endurance to the uttermost. He had been prepared, at the cost of severe mental conflict, to meet one of the most cruel emergencies of life, and no such emergency had occurred.

The meeting had been large and specially pervaded by a genial New Year influence. The ordinary business was gone through with less friction than usual, the quiet tact and courtesy of the Rector unconsciously emitting rays of irresistible influence.

No one could have guessed, who marked the unruffled patience with which he expounded the minute and tedious matters of business under discussion, and submitted to the frequent interruptions and contradictions with which statement and suggestion were encountered, that an almost intolerable anxiety was gnawing at his heart—no one, at least, who was not a very keen physiognomist.

But time went on : accounts were duly examined and passed : resolutions of the narrowest parochial interest proposed and seconded,—amongst them the vote of thanks to himself,—but still his enemy did not appear. What could it mean?

Had he after all relented at the eleventh

hour, his better nature getting the mastery? Or was it the result of some unforeseen accident, or a deliberate snare to cheat him into false security?

At least it was a reprieve for which he thanked God devoutly; not so much for his own deliverance as for the joy and comfort it was now in his power to take back to the beloved, suffering wife at home.

As soon as he could civilly shake himself free from his friends, he walked home at a rapid pace. The two hours' absence he had mentioned, as the term of the meeting, had been considerably extended, and the unusual excitement and prostration of Sybil had filled him with a vague and depressing apprehension.

As he came within sight of his own house he saw Jack and Tom standing in the open doorway. As soon as they recognised him they rushed down the steps to meet him.

'We are only just come in,' said Jack, 'and we found the morning performance at the Gaiety very flat after Covent Garden last night; we did not stop to the end. We were on the look-out for you, not knowing what to do with ourselves. We wondered to find Sybil gone out, when she seemed quite ill this morning. Of course she will be back to dinner?'

'Sybil out!' repeated Julian in a tone of stupefaction; but even as he spoke a sense of some immeasurable calamity swept over his mind. Was the explanation already awaiting him of her profound emotion and Gilbert Helstone's failure of execution? As was habitual to him, he succeeded in maintaining his outward composure.

'You are only just come home,' he said to the boys, 'and cannot have made sure she is not there.'

They were quite sure; they had gone into every room of the house to look for her.

He went into the house without another word, entered the library, and looked round for some hint of explanation. There was none, unless it were the crimson coverlet which lay in a heap on the floor. He searched the writing table to see if there were any letter or written scrap of paper in her handwriting, but found nothing. Then suddenly catching sight of his own white face and distended eyes in a glass, a reaction of feeling occurred. Why was he mad enough to give way to this nameless and intolerable dread, when perhaps the simplest explanation was at hand? Sybil's panacea for a headache was the open air—she had probably gone out for a walk or drive. He rang the bell to question the servants, but even as he thus tried to reassure himself the same deep-rooted misgiving mocked his efforts.

The man who answered the bell replied that Mrs. Karslake had gone out about an hour or so after the master himself, but he was not in the house at the time, and he thought the parlour-maid could give further particulars. It was evident to Karslake that he spoke with reluctance, and he was conscious of an expression of intelligent sympathy in the man's face, that brought back the sensitive colour into his own.

The girl, who also acted occasionally as Sybil's maid, was then called; she was bursting with anxiety to tell her story.

A letter, she said, had been brought to Mrs. Karslake almost immediately after his own departure. She had taken it into the library herself, and her mistress was then lying on the sofa. She told her to put it down on the table, not knowing that an answer was expected; but when she understood the messenger was waiting, she bade the servant leave the room, and she would ring when she was ready. It was a very long time indeed, perhaps half an hour, before the bell was rung ; when she went in again the letter was lying on the table in a sealed envelope but without any address. She did not see Mrs. Karslake's face at all, for she was lying on the sofa with her head turned to the wall, and buried in the pillow. She took out the letter and gave it to the messenger ; she did not know who he was, or where he came from.

Presently she heard her mistress go up-stairs, and then her dressing-room bell rang. She told her she was suddenly called away from home, and ordered her to pack a small tin travelling-case with necessary clothes. She thought she understood her to say for a month's absence, but was not quite sure and did not like to ask any questions. Mrs. Karslake would only let her put in a few of her plainest dresses and no ornaments of any kind; she was not crying but dreadfully white and still.

When the box was ready it was taken down into the hall, and almost at the same moment a cab drove up to the door; there was no one in the cab. Then Mrs. Karslake came down-stairs, dressed for a journey; she went into the library again and stayed there a little while, perhaps ten minutes. Then she came out, said 'good-bye' in a very faint voice to her and the man-servant in attendance, got into the cab, and was driven away. She knew nothing more.

'What orders were given to the cabman?' asked Karslake, in a voice calm indeed, but so strained and unnatural as to be scarcely recognisable.

Mrs. Karslake had said no orders were required; the man knew where to go.

'And she left no letter—no message?'

'None;' she answered, and then the girl

burst out crying, and Karslake motioned to them to leave the room.

But he was not to be allowed the privilege of solitude at present. The moment the servants had left the room the boys knocked for admission, and there was no alternative but to bid them come in. The sight of their pale, scared faces was another pang : what was he to say to them?

Jack was generally spokesman.

'We want to know where Sybil is?' and there was a touch of sullenness and suspicion in his manner. 'You must know all about it, and where she is gone! What is wrong all on a sudden, and why was the girl crying?'

'It is very natural that you should think I must know all about it, but the fact is I am as much taken by surprise as you in not finding her at home on my return. At present I cannot discuss the matter, and must ask you to leave me alone for a little while, that I may be able to think it out by myself.'

The boys looked at one another as if for encouragement. Then Tom spoke:

'We fancy it is something to do with what she saw at Covent Garden that night—don't you know of anything that made her unhappy?'

He hesitated: it was hard to run this childish gauntlet.

'I cannot answer you, Tom. I am not able to talk it over with you now.'

He went to the door and opened it for their departure.

'You must understand that I am in trouble and want to be alone. When dinner is ready sit down and manage by yourselves; don't wait for me.'

Whatever the acuteness of his mental suffering, he did not betray it by symptoms open to the boys' penetration. They could not read aright the lines of strained endurance in his face, but they could remark that the voice in which he spoke was clear and steady, and it raised a spirit of resistance in Tom's mind.

'If I were a man instead of a boy you would be obliged to discuss the matter with me! But father will want to understand.'

To this Karslake made no reply; he still stood with the door in his hand as if waiting to shut them out. They felt there was nothing else to be done but to go, and they walked slowly past him with sullen averted faces.

Then for a few moments he stood still in the same spot, and involuntarily raised his hands to his head, which throbbed now with physical pain. If ever a man saw himself standing alone and desolate in life, with all his household hopes shattered around him, it was he; and for a time he felt he must hold thought in suspense lest he should not have the courage to face his necessity. Presently his eyes fell on the little table that had been pushed on one side, so cruelly suggestive of the incidents of the early morning, and on the couch where she had lain, and he felt impelled to fling himself prone on the latter and surrender his manhood in tears, without further conflict of repression ; but he did not yield to the impulse. The coercion of duty and self-control becomes in a sense mechanical over minds pledged to constant obedience ; and Karslake walked slowly back to the fire and sat down in his accustomed chair to think over what was next and wisest to be done. No slightest doubt of his wife's honour or his wife's devotion passed through his mind ; rather he dimly guessed at once there must be some connection between her absence and Helstone's discarded vengeance. What perplexed him was how and when they had communicated with each other since his own visit to the Temple the day before.

All the pathetic tenderness and intense agitation of the morning were to be fully explained, on the supposition that she had then decided on her sacrificial act of desertion. But what means had she employed to let their enemy know that she was willing to pay the redemption price demanded? Another thought occurred. What must be the relentless nature of the man who could extort from the magnanimous devotion of a wife such a supreme sacrifice? But he turned deliberately from the latter consideration; it was unwise to fan into a flame the natural fires of hate and vengeance; rather would he fortify his mind with the thought of the divine unselfishness of Sybil's love. There was consolation and incentive to patience and endurance in the future in this alone, and, for the rest, of course he would

win her back to him ; that result was only a
question of time. He would prove to her con-
clusively that the disgrace she averted was but
a fictitious shame, not for a moment to be
weighed in the balance against the solace of
her love ; and that even if the humiliation had
been absolute, they were bound, by the sacred
obligation of their marriage vows, to stand by
each other through good and evil fortune.

Then it occurred to him he did not know
for certain how Sybil had passed the preceding
evening after she had left him, and that he had
felt a measure of surprise at her absenting
herself through the entire length of it. At
least on this point her brothers could inform
him, and he left the room at once to find and
question them.

Dinner was cleared away, and there was
some dessert on the table : but neither Jack
nor Tom had touched it. They were sitting

both together in a roomy lounging-chair pulled
close to the hot fire, with their arms round
each other, in the loose embrace which was an
habitual attitude with them, and their voices
dropped in low, earnest talk.   They looked up
in rather a shame-faced fashion as Karslake
entered.   In answer to his inquiries as to
whether Sybil had spent the whole of the preceding evening in their company, he received
of course an emphatic negative.

'We thought she was with you in the
library,' said Jack.   'She went in there after
dinner, and we never saw her again till breakfast time this morning.'

It was becoming abundantly clear to his
mind.   She had gone to make a last appeal to
Gilbert Helstone, and had accepted his terms
of deliverance ; and he himself—absorbed in
what now seemed to him a selfish pre-occupation—had suffered her to pass the hours of her

struggle and anguish alone—at what a cost had
been sufficiently indicated by her manner and
appearance that morning. Surely he must
have been blind and insensible not to have
read those signs aright! The momentous
question was what had become of her? what
place of refuge or plan of concealment had
been dictated to her? He would go and see
Helstone at once, and compel him to give up
what information was in his power.

CHAPTER XXX.

HE went out of the house without telling the
boys where he was going, and equally without
any consideration of the pain and humiliation
to which he might be subjected. To find
some degree of rest in ceaseless movement was
the natural craving of his present mood;
repose, either of body or mind, seemed impossible under the pressure of his cruel distress.

It was much the same hour and same
weather—fog and drizzling rain—as on the
preceding night, when Sybil had turned her
steps in the same direction; and in like manner, on hearing the sound of his inquiries in
the hall, Sara Helstone opened the door of the

room where she was sitting, and came out to speak to him. In his case, however, there was no friendly recognition or welcome.

She dismissed the servant with a gesture before she opened her lips, and even then she looked at him for a few moments in silence, with an expression at once eager and dissatisfied. A sudden breathless hope glanced across his mind.

'Is my wife—is Sybil here?' he gasped.

Sara gave a short laugh. 'Come in here with me,' she said, 'if I must speak to you, which I would much rather not. Do not let anyone hear the sound of your voice!'

He followed her into the room, she closing the door carefully behind them with a pre-occupied and restless manner. She seemed to bring her mind with difficulty to the subject before her, and he was obliged to repeat his inquiry ere she seemed fully to follow his meaning.

'Sybil!' she said vaguely, at last, 'she was here last night, and I walked home with her. I know nothing since.'

'You did not know she had left my house this morning?'

There was something in his tone and manner that at length had the effect of arresting her attention; she brought her gaze to bear consciously upon him, and her face softened a little.

'I will not tell you a lie,' she answered; 'so much as that I know, but where she is now or what led her to take such a step I do not. But you, I presume, have not to go very far for the solution of the mystery?'

'The solution of the mystery is a man's thirst for mistaken vengeance and a woman's power of sacrificing love.'

'So be it!' she answered with renewed impatience. 'I have neither time nor inclination just now to discuss this point. I tell you again I have no information to give you, and just now my mind is so harassed by private anxiety that you will pardon my telling you plainly I should like to be alone. To-morrow, perhaps, when my brother is in town, if it will be any satisfaction to you to see me again, I shall be more at liberty.'

He turned to depart at once, then stopped

'I will intrude no longer on you, but if Mr. Helstone is at home, I cannot leave the house without seeing him. You must understand that my suspense is almost more than I can bear.'

'You cannot by any possibility see Gilbert to-night, and on my honour he could not relieve your anxiety. He knows no more than myself where Mrs. Karslake is.'

Her eagerness to be quit of his presence was so overmastering that she even laid her hand on his arm to urge his departure; there was no resource but to yield. He took up his hat and went out into the hall, Sara following him in anxious attendance; but before he had reached the street door, there was a sudden rush of confused tempestuous sound from the upper stories of the house. Sara's face blanched to deadly pallor; he instinctively stood still.

'What is that?' he demanded, scarcely able to analyse the impression produced.

Before she could answer a door from above burst open, and a woman appeared on the head of the stairs, leaning breathlessly over the balusters to the hall below, and beckoning for help with a restrained but imperative gesture. Scarcely considering what he did Karslake sprang up the stairs to her side.

'What is wrong? can I be of use?' he asked.

The woman, who had a powerful frame and

arm of iron, glanced at him for a moment with keen doubtful scrutiny, but her movements though heavy were prompt and decisive.

'At least you can try,' she answered, in a harsh guttural voice, retreating rapidly as she spoke towards the door she had just quitted, and whence issued sounds of inarticulate fury.

'We want help,' she continued; 'go in and do your best; for God's sake part them if you can, before murder is done! A strange face and voice may divert her attention. I am no longer of any use!'

Karslake followed her without question or hesitation. The room he entered was dimly lighted by a lamp hung close to the ceiling, and the rays of which were further absorbed by the gloomy padded walls and thick dark carpet on the floor. Directly beneath the rays of this lamp, so as to bring their features and figures into ghastly relief, a man and woman were locked together in what was evidently a mortal struggle. The woman was tall and spare in form, but one glance was enough to see that the convulsive clutch with which she grasped the other's throat was the irresistible strength of madness. Her long gray tresses of hair, still abundant, floated over her shoulders, and the lines of her face and the · tones of her voice were inflamed with irresponsible fury, as she succeeded in straitening her suffocating hold in spite of the powerful resistance of her victim.

It was a sickening spectacle ; Helstone's livid face and distended eyes showing the extremity of his condition.

The situation, which takes time to describe, was instantaneously apprehended by Karslake. He perceived at a glance that any attempt to tear the maniac from her prey must fail fatally, and with a swift movement he advanced in front of her, so as to stand in the full focus of her raised vision, and rolling up the handkerchief he held in his hand, threw it suddenly, and with all the force of which the action admitted, into her face.

As he expected, with a cry of brutal rage she released her hold of Helstone, and precipitated herself upon him. But he was not only prepared for the attack, but had all the nerve and training of a young English athlete, also the advantage of considerably greater height. He succeeded in evading the snatch of her desperate fingers; the keeper at the same time rushing forward to secure her patient, but not before the mad woman had, by an unexpected movement, seized his hand, and bitten it through to the bone.

Karslake stooped to pick up his handkerchief, in order to wrap it round the wound; partly also to hide the involuntary contraction of pain. As he rose he met Helstone's eyes fixed upon him with an expression difficult to define, but in which gratitude or recognition obviously had no part.

'Let us go,' he said hoarsely, rising with difficulty from the chair into which he had fallen; 'the paroxysm is over—she will be able to manage her now.'

The struggle had been an exhausting one. He staggered a little as he turned, and tried to walk with his usual independence of gait and gesture.

Karslake came up to him and offered his arm.

'Forget that we are enemies,' he said; 'at least, till I have seen you safe under your sister's care.'

Helstone's face turned deadly pale. 'This is too much,' he said; 'my punishment is greater than I can bear. I would rather have lost my life than have owed it to you. I can manage without help.'

Outside the door, which the nurse had forcibly locked against her, stood Sara leaning against the wall. She drew a deep gasping sigh as she recognised her brother's safety, but an imperative movement on his part seemed to check the words she would have spoken.

Helstone slowly led the way down-stairs, and then turned into the dining-room. 'I must speak to Julian Karslake alone,' he said, and Sara withdrew in silence to her room opposite.

The wine still stood on the table. He went up to it, half filled a tumbler, and drained it to the bottom.

'Will you drink?' he asked, but Karslake shook his head.

'You will not drink nor sit in my house,' resumed Helstone, in the same tone of bitter cynicism as before, 'but for all that I must

detain you for a moment. You must promise
me to keep the miserable secret that circumstances have revealed to you to-night. My
honour is pledged to keep that desperate
woman under my own roof—you will not
betray me?'

'No, I will not betray you.'

'One word more. I freely own I owe
my life to your courage and self-possession,
qualities in which I never thought you defi-
cient; but I can profess no gratitude. It is a
pain deeper than words can tell, that you
should have seen what you have seen to-night,
and laid me under this obligation. If you
know human nature, you will easily understand
that I love you none the better for it. You do
not think to buy off my enmity thus?'

'My action was without calculation or any
recognition of your own personality—there is
no question of obligation between us. Shall

we consider that point settled? I have something to say in my turn.'

He leaned heavily against the table as he spoke. The suspended rush of his own anguish, added to the strain of protracted physical and mental exhaustion, and the renewed necessity of self-repression in the presence of his heartless foe, seemed almost beyond his strength. Helstone sat and watched him with relentless scrutiny, with which a sense of unwilling admiration slowly mingled.

'You are sick with pain,' he said, rising and pouring out a glass of water, 'though I own you have borne it well. I know of old she has the fangs of a tigress—drink this! No? As you please, but it is a pity to balk the first movement of charity I ever felt in your behalf.'

'It is a greater pity I think,' replied Karslake coldly, 'to waste time by the wearisome iteration of your sentiments towards myself.

I came here to-night to ask you what has become of my wife, and I will not go away without an answer.'

'Oh, you shall have your answer!—I do not know. I have not the slightest clue to her present whereabouts. You do not believe me? In that case both for your sake and my own, we will end the interview.'

He rose as he spoke, as if to intimate his intention of leaving the room, but Karslake intercepted him.

'I know she came to you last night, to speak in my behalf, and I conclude you forced her to this desperate alternative by working upon her feelings in a way that your knowledge of her character would well fit you to do. But the practical details of her secret departure were never arranged by herself, and I come to you for the information that no one else can give.'

'We often come for what we cannot get,'

was the sneering reply, ' and in this case, had I the best will in the world, I could not help you. Not that I would help you if I could! Your love for your wife has much of the shamelessness of your love for your mistress ; you would keep her at any cost of dishonour. But such is not her way of looking at things—she decided of her own free-will to leave you. Love without respect was impossible to Sybil Dorrimore. Have I not told you I would encourage her to bear misery rather than shame? Well, I have fulfilled my threat, and broken the cursed bond between you.'

Karslake was silent for a few moments. Then he said :

' The one object I had in view in coming here to-night is lost, if I am to believe what you say ; and for the rest, I am constitutionally fortified against abusive language, and am not tempted to unburden my mind of my personal

sentiments, as you are.   Equally do I refuse to
dispute your explanation of the motives that have
influenced Mrs. Karslake.   Enough that, even
in the first keenness of my loss, I can find some
comfort in the thought of the loving magnanimity which has inflicted it: your vindictiveness,
after all, can only go a certain length.'

'Have you done?' interrupted Helstone.
'I forbear to reply or threaten, for your wife
has purchased future immunity for you so long
as she keeps, as she probably will keep, her part
of the bond.   Shall I suggest that you should go
home, if such a word is any longer applicable
to S. Mark's Rectory?   If you feel no necessity
for pulling yourself together after the events of
the night, I do.'

He laid his hand on the bell.   The events of
the night, Karslake's invincible self-command
under provocation, his own repeated failure to
provoke him to protest or recrimination, or to

humble him to admission or complaint, only served as a stimulus to his malice and hatred, and exasperated him almost beyond observing the decency of social restraints.   And now to be added to the score were the unpayable service he had rendered him, and a corroding anxiety he could not bring himself to express.   He had a morbid dread of discovery and interference with the miserable secret of his household, but when Karslake got home, would he not summon doctor or servant to dress his lacerated and ignoble wound, and by so doing provoke inquiry and speculation? Must he stoop to solicitation on this point?

Julian had turned already to depart.

'It is unnecessary to ring the bell,' he said, in reply to his host's doubtful courtesy; 'I shall prefer to dismiss myself.'

Helstone followed him into the hall.

'One more word,' he said, in the harsh,

reluctant accents of a man who speaks against the grain. 'I am scarcely brute enough to let you leave the house without acknowledging again the debt I owe you. It will make no difference in our relations—understand that clearly, but it exists. Another: my sister is an excellent surgeon; will you not let her see your hurt and prescribe for it before you go? Your servant or doctor might ask questions that would compromise your pledge.'

'I can keep a pledge, even under difficulties,' replied Karslake coldly. 'Do not be uneasy, it is the left hand; there will be no need of assistance; no one shall see it but myself. Good-night.'

END OF THE SECOND VOLUME.

Spottiswoode & Co. Printers, New-street Square, London.

UNIFORM EDITION OF

MRS. GASKELL'S NOVELS AND TALES.

In Seven Volumes, each containing Four Illustrations.

Price 3s. 6d. each bound in cloth, or in Sets of Seven Volumes, handsomely bound in half-morocco, price £2. 10s.

CONTENTS OF THE VOLUMES

VOL. I.
WIVES AND DAUGHTERS.

VOL. II.
NORTH AND SOUTH.

VOL. III.
SYLVIA'S LOVERS.

VOL. IV.
CRANFORD.

COMPANY MANNERS.
THE WELL OF PEN-MORPHA.
THE HEART OF JOHN MIDDLETON.
TRAITS AND STORIES OF THE HUGUENOTS.
SIX WEEKS AT HEPPENHEIM.
THE SQUIRE'S STORY.
LIBBIE MARSH'S THREE ERAS.

CURIOUS IF TRUE.
THE MOORLAND COTTAGE.
THE SEXTON'S HERO.
DISAPPEARANCES.
RIGHT AT LAST.
THE MANCHESTER MARRIAGE.
LOIS, THE WITCH.
THE CROOKED BRANCH.

VOL. V.
MARY BARTON.

COUSIN PHILLIS.
MY FRENCH MASTER.
THE OLD NURSE'S STORY.

BESSY'S TROUBLES AT HOME.
CHRISTMAS STORMS AND SUNSHINE

VOL. VI.
RUTH.

THE GREY WOMAN.
MORTON HALL.

MR. HARRISON'S CONFESSIONS.
HAND AND HEART.

VOL. VII.
LIZZIE LEIGH.

A DARK NIGHT'S WORK.
ROUND THE SOFA.
MY LADY LUDLOW.
AN ACCURSED RACE.

THE DOOM OF THE GRIFFITHS.
HALF A LIFETIME AGO.
THE POOR CLARE.
THE HALF-BROTHERS.

London : SMITH, ELDER, & CO., 15 Waterloo Place.

www.ingramcontent.com/pod-product-compliance
Lightning Source LLC
Chambersburg PA
CBHW020849020726
47497CB00005B/1322